## "Don't the women so easily these d

Jet was feeling light-headed and reckless as the car pulled to a halt in front of the house. "It was a very different story six years ago with me, wasn't it? And by the way, how *did* you manage to get rid of your fiancée then? With your usual callousness, I imagine."

She slid out of the car and into the blessedly cool night air, puzzled by his lack of response. It made her feel apprehensive. She slammed the car door shut and hurried to let herself into the house.

There was no sound of following footsteps as she closed the door behind her, but her heart began to thud as she listened for the sound of the Porsche's engine.

Suddenly the door behind her moved, and she scrambled round to hurl her weight against it—too late....

**DIANA HAMILTON** creates high-tension conflict that brings new life to traditional romance. Readers will no doubt find her a welcome addition to the Harlequin Presents program, and will be glad to know that more novels by this talented author are already in the works.

# DIANA HAMILTON

## song in a strange land

**Harlequin Books**

TORONTO • NEW YORK • LONDON
AMSTERDAM • PARIS • SYDNEY • HAMBURG
STOCKHOLM • ATHENS • TOKYO • MILAN

Harlequin Presents first edition July 1987
ISBN 0-373-10993-8

Original hardcover edition published in 1986
by Mills & Boon Limited

# CHAPTER ONE

JET LUELLYN swung the big silver limousine off the motorway at the Telford intersection. She disliked the boredom of motorway driving, and her slim, capable hands relaxed a little on the wheel as she took the road to Ironbridge.

Negotiating the traffic on the narrow main street took all her attention. The historic little town was in holiday mood, knots of slow-moving foreign tourists with cameras slung around their necks everywhere, local housewives hurrying along with shopping bags, sunlight glinting on the Severn to her left, the swell of spring floodwaters pushing the river through the thickly wooded gorge at a turbulent rate.

She considered stopping for coffee. Breakfast back at her London apartment seemed a very long time ago. Barbie, her live-in secretary-cum-Girl Friday, had told her, 'Have a good break, Jet, you deserve it', following her remark with a quick warm smile then turning her attention to the child. Ben, Barbie's almost-five-year-old son, had been eating cereal with an owl-eyed solemnity that belied his infinite capacity for mischief.

Jet tightened her lips to a long scarlet line above a neatly determined chin and gave up the idea of coffee. It seemed impossible to find a parking space, and she would soon be home.

Home. How long was it since she had thought of Foundlands, high in the Shropshire border hills, as home? How long since she had thought of it at all?

Her startlingly blue eyes narrowed between thick

fringes of dark lashes. Six years. She had cut Foundlands, Uncle Micah and twelve years of her life right out of her thoughts six years ago, the amputation carried out with a surgeon-like precision.

Now Micah was dead. He had willed Foundlands, the small hill farm, and its few remaining acres, to Alan Taylor, his godson. And a week ago Alan had phoned and said, 'I'm putting Foundlands up for auction now that probate's through. Want to come up and see the old place before it goes under the hammer?'

Alan was twenty-five, a year older than Jet, and he'd spent part of the school holidays with his godfather each summer while Jet had been living there. She and Alan had always got along well together, and since Micah had thrown Jet out, six years back, they had kept in touch. Just simple messages on cards each Christmas, relaying what news there was, and once Alan had stayed overnight at her London apartment just off Temple Street, meeting Barbie and Ben and getting on with them as comfortably as he got on with anyone who didn't actually punch him in the eye.

And six years on Jet was tough enough, controlled enough to take a last look at her former home without turning a hair. She wouldn't have agreed to make the trip if she hadn't been sure of that.

'You need a complete break,' Barbie had said, her expression as severe as bouncy red curls, a tip-tilted nose and curvy mouth would let it be. 'Go away and see your nice friend Alan and don't even think of work for a week. It's more than time you took a holiday.'

'We were in France last autumn,' Jet pointed out, surprised that Barbie should remember Alan.

'So?' Barbie dismissed that. 'That was research for the book you've just finished. You didn't relax for one minute.'

Jet didn't believe in letting herself relax. A relaxed mind could let forbidden memories in under its guard. She thrived on hard work. Hard work paid dividends. Six fast-paced, intricately plotted, hard-bitten crime novels had given her a bank balance that never ceased to quietly amaze her. Her novels, published under the pen name of Roger Blye, had soared to international bestsellerdom; two had already been made into films and her agent was currently negotiating an even better contract for the sale of the film rights on two more. Her popularity as a novelist was rising as hard and as fast as her style, but she didn't get big-headed about it; she took it as calmly as she took everything else.

Her work was all she needed. And if there'd been a match-making look in Barbie's brown eyes then she was wasting her time. Alan was a dear friend—they went way back—and Jet had no intention of allowing herself to get romantically involved with him or anyone else. Love was too painful an emotion to admit into her scheme of things. She had grown a protective shell around her heart a mile thick. Jet was self-confessedly as hard as nails, as tough as old boots. It hadn't always been so . . . but that was something she never thought about now.

As she drove west the lanes grew steeper, narrower. Late April sunlight gilded the green flanks of hills that shouldered a harebell blue sky patterned with puffy white clouds. The hill village of Tipper's Batch showed through a haze of budding oak trees, and Jet drove slowly down the only street, past the huddle of grey stone cottages and the Victorian primary school where her uncle had sent her on the day after she'd gone to live with him.

Her mouth had a wry twist to it as the only visible inhabitants of Tipper's Batch—an old man with a wheelbarrow and two women gossiping over a fence—

stared at the passing BMW. No one would relate the young woman with the cool pale face behind the wheel to the wild haired, frantic-eyed six-year-old who'd been pushed through the school doors eighteen years ago by an uncle who had no time for her.

Foundlands was a mile and a half out of the village. It was a long, stone-built farmhouse with twisted roofs, hugging the hillside. Jet drove the BMW down the pot-holed approach track with care, noticing, as she drew nearer, the ramshackle state of the clustered outbuildings, the peeling paintwork and missing slates of the farmhouse, the rank weeds growing out of the mud of the yard. Foundlands had never been well kept, but Micah had obviously let things slip even further during latter years.

But there was a plume of smoke rising from one of the chimneys, blown almost horizontal by the prevailing west wind—an angle echoed by the stunted thorn trees that sheltered the main house—and a mud-spattered Land Rover parked near the barn. Alan.

Her long, beautifully shaped mouth curved in a slow smile. It would be good to see him again. And no sooner had she cut the engine and reached for her leather shoulder bag than he was opening the door at her side.

'This your new toy?' His light grey eyes swept appreciatively over the sleek bodywork of the car.

'You could call it that.'

'Very fancy.'

'That, too.' Jet slid long, shapely silk-clad legs to the ground, emerging gracefully to stand beside him. 'I like the best.'

She bought quality because it gave better service, and she could afford it now. That principle showed in the cashmere and wool coffee-coloured skirt she wore with a cream silk shirt, cream cashmere jacket and hand-made Italian leather shoes.

Jet was tall for a woman, fine-boned and slender, the top of her glossy dark head, its thick length of hair coiled immaculately into her nape, on a level with Alan's crinkly light brown curls.

'It's great to see you, Jet. You're looking better each time.'

His warm, blunt-fingered hand clasped her cool, long fingers, swallowing them in his calloused palm, and Jet gave him her rare warm smile, one finely arched brow raised in question.

'Better-looking, I mean.' Alan's face went brick red, his weathered features and stocky build a product of generations of farming people. 'Come inside; I'll get some tea brewing.'

The inside of the house was a mess. Jet had tried to keep it reasonably clean when she'd lived here. But what could one do when the few pieces of furniture were the cheapest and meanest available and her efforts were sourly pronounced a waste of time by an old misogynist who thought home comforts 'womanish'?

Jet shrugged; the place looked as if it hadn't been cleaned since she'd left.

She sat on a wooden kitchen chair near the old-fashioned range and watched Alan take the battered old black kettle from the fire and pour boiling water over the tea leaves in the big brown pot, his hands deft for all their clumsy appearance.

'Raise any ghosts?' he asked her, tipping his head to indicate the drab, sparsely furnished living-room, the overhead beams thickly festooned with cobwebs.

'None.'

As far as Jet was concerned there were no ghosts to be raised. There was a self-imposed gap in her life that

began when she was a six-year-old orphan being handed
over to her only relative, Uncle Micah, and ended after
the death of her son just over fourteen years later. She
had cut the intervening years out of her life, a process
that had been frighteningly simple when a steel-cold
hardness had petrified her soul after baby Tod's death.

So sitting in this room didn't bring back memories of
long, cold winter nights when a lonely child had played
with a doll she'd codged together out of bits of stick and
rag, or in later years, sat at the deal table poring over the
hated farm accounts.

'Glad to hear it.' He handed her a mug of strong, hot
tea. 'Old Micah was a damned old bastard where you
were concerned. God! Sorry——' A dull flush of
discomfiture poured a rapid stain over his features. 'I
didn't mean anything——'

'Forget it,' Jet told him, sipping tea, her dark sapphire
eyes steady over the rim of her mug as she watched him
struggle with his embarrassment.

'I only mean, well, it would be a pity if you couldn't
enjoy some of your memories, wouldn't it?' he muttered.
'We had some rare times together when we were kids,
though it must have been hell for you the rest of the year,
alone here with him. Even now I have to laugh over some
of the things we got up to—I always used to look forward
to spending a couple of weeks here in the summer; you
were such a crazy kid in those days——'

Alan was normally shy, inarticulate, and he was doing
his best now to cover his slip of the tongue. Strange—the
thought flashed unbidden and unwanted into Jet's
mind—strange how she'd never once thought of Tod as a
bastard. But he had been, of course.

The iron shutter that separated that part of her life
from her consciousness came down with the abrupt
precision of total self-control, and her voice was cool and

clear, her smile untroubled as she put her mug aside and asked him, 'When's the auction?'

'A week today. The estate agent bod thought it the best way of getting shot of the place.' He threw more logs on the range and wiped his hands down the sides of his cord pants before tipping a pile of yellowing newspapers off a stool and pulling it closer to her, sitting down. 'I don't reckon there'll be much interest in the place. One chap's made some enquiries—he'll be at the auction. But I might as well have sold privately to him, I reckon, for all the interest there'll be when it's public.'

'You didn't consider keeping it?'

Alan pulled a face. 'The house and buildings would be a liability, and the bit of land that's left over is more than twenty miles from my place. Not worth hanging on to, stands to reason.'

Alan had taken over the family farm in Corve Dale after the death of his father a few years back, he wouldn't want to be bothered with Foundlands. Getting to her feet, Jet collected the empty mugs and put them on the table.

'Is your mother well?'

'Middling: she still misses Dad. While you're up here, perhaps you could find time to visit her? She'd like that.'

'I'll make time.' She had seen Alan's parents when they'd driven over to bring Alan for his holidays with Micah, collecting him when it was over, staying to chat for a while. Jet had liked them and had known instinctively that they were a devoted couple. She had envied Alan his good family life. Her own parents had died when she was six and her sole relative, her father's much older brother, had made it clear, right from day one, that he hadn't wanted her.

Jet went to the small-paned window and stared out at the view across the valley, saying as Alan came to join

her, 'If those outbuildings were pulled down, the view
from the front of the house would be superb.'

'Oh—I suppose so.' Alan could take a breathcatching
view, or leave it. The enchanting quality of the border
hill land had never taken hold of his soul as it had Jet's.
'You won't be travelling back to London tonight, will
you? So how about if I fix you up with a room at the
village pub? I didn't want to arrange anything without
asking you first; I didn't know what your plans were.'

'What are you doing?'

'Me?' Alan shrugged, his powerful shoulders seeming
huge under his tweed jacket, his stockiness making her
slender height contrastingly fragile. 'I'll be kipping down
here for a couple of nights; I've got to go through the old
man's things.'

'Mind if I stay, too?' Jet didn't fancy the local pub. It
wasn't that she couldn't face the slyly interested looks,
the questions of locals who might recognise her and
remember. She simply couldn't be bothered to parry
them. And if she stayed here she could help Alan with
what could prove to be a depressing and monumental
job.

Alan's mother had packed enough food to feed him for a
fortnight instead of the two days he intended to stay at
Foundlands. Jet grilled two steaks on the grimy electric
cooker in the squalid kitchen and smiled slightly as she
thought of how Alan had made up a bed for her in the
spare room. He was using Micah's old room and had,
tactfully, decided she was not to sleep in the small square
bedroom that had been hers for twelve years. She hadn't
argued with him; it was immaterial to her which room
she used. She wasn't afraid to face memories because she
didn't allow them to intrude. Ever. Alan didn't realise
how hard she had become; he still imbued her with the

sensitivity of the girl he had known many years ago.

'This place should have come to you, by rights,' he told her as they ate. 'You were his only blood relative.'

'He disliked and resented me—why should he have been expected to leave me anything? Tell me about yourself.' She turned the subject to something more interesting. 'No thoughts yet of getting married and giving your mother the grandchildren she's longing for?'

As soon as she saw his face pinch up with embarrassment she could have bitten her tongue out. The trouble was, she'd learned to forget—learned too well, perhaps, at least in this instance.

She should have remembered how he had come to her in that grotty flat she'd been sharing with Denise, and had asked her to marry him. He'd loved her for a long time, he'd muttered, shyness making him stumble over the words. He knew she didn't love him, not in that way, but he'd make her happy, be damned if he wouldn't. And he'd give the child she was carrying a name and be a proper father to it, since its real father didn't give a damn.

Alan speared a piece of meat and pushed it into his mouth, chewing stoically, his head down to hide the cringing look in his eyes.

Annoyed with herself for her own thoughtlessness, Jet talked of neutral matters, eventually managing to draw an easy response to her question, 'How much land did Micah sell off over the years?'

'Most of it.' He put his cutlery down and leaned back, replete and relaxed again, the embarrassment evoked by the memory of his single declaration of love, his offer to marry her and her grateful but determined rejection, over now. 'Manny Granger from Town Farm bought the lower meadows and the stretch of the sheep walks that runs from Mere End to Crow's Top. And that chap I was telling you about, who's keen to buy this place, bought Tipper's Hollow and the strip of woodland by the stream—oh, three, four years back. He wanted it for a weekend cottage—fair transformed the place.'

'Good Lord!' Jet remembered the near-derelict cottage on the edge of her uncle's land; she had played there often enough as a child. It had once been occupied, but the shepherd who'd lived there had been long gone by the time Jet had come to Foundlands, her uncle preferring to manage the flocks on his own, saving the hired man's wages. She couldn't imagine the broken little house being a comfortable weekend home.

'I wonder why he wants to buy this place as well,' Jet mused idly, the cool purity of her features displaying only a slight amount of academic interest.

'Beats me. Fancy some coffee?' Alan went to the range, pushing the kettle over the hottest part of the fire, reaching for a jar of instant coffee and two mugs from the cluttered dresser. 'He's already got Tipper's Hollow for himself, and he can't be interested in the bit of land that goes with this place—it's nothing but bog and whin. Maybe he wants to convert it for other holidaymakers, let it out to trippers at a fat rent.'

'Maybe.' Jet stifled a yawn, losing interest. It had been a long day.

She slept well, as she always did, but there was something deeply satisfying about waking up to the sound of birdsong and the background voice of the hill stream as it chattered to itself on its stony bed behind the house.

Pulling a pair of superbly tailored trousers and a matching slate grey single-breasted jacket with long, narrow lapels from her weekend case, she vaguely regretted her lack of more casual clothes. During the twelve years she'd lived here she'd worn nothing but jeans or cords, T-shirts or sweaters, all either much too big for her or too small. Some she'd bought at rummage sales, others had been Alan's hand-me-downs donated from time to time by his mother who must have been shocked by the disreputable state of the black-haired, gipsy-like child who ran wild on her uncle's lands—and anyone else's within roaming distance.

From time to time there had been mutterings in the village about the way young Jet Luellyn was left to run wild. Some said she'd been dragged up, others that there was no 'dragged up' about it, she'd simply been left to fend for herself, like a wild thing.

There was no trace of that former wildness in the reflection that presented itself to Jet that morning. The discoloured mirror showed a tall, graceful figure, the immaculately cut trouser suit discreetly emphasising the small rounded breasts, neat waist and slender hips above long elegant legs. The blue silk scarf casually knotted around her slim neck complemented the colour of her remarkable eyes, and the cool, pale face with its exquisitely modelled features spoke only of composure. Only the fullness of the wide lower lip hinted at passions long subdued.

Jet patted the glossy, dark coil of hair at her nape, satisfying herself that no stray tendrils escaped, then left her room and made her way down the narrow, uncarpeted stairs. The aroma of frying bacon told her that Alan was up and busy. After poking her nose into the awful kitchen and saying good morning, she went to the sitting-room and covered the grubby deal table with the most presentable cloth she could find, then hunted through a dresser drawer for cutlery.

Sunlight was streamimg through the little window, laying a drift of gold wherever it fell, and Jet suddenly felt in a rare holiday mood. With a little modernisation and a great amount of cleaning up, this place could be made into a pleasant retreat. There would be peace and quiet for her work, and young Ben would benefit from the clean country air and the freedom of the wide open spaces. Barbie, too, would enjoy Foundlands. She had been born and brought up in the country and had often said she found London claustrophobic.

Unconsciously, Jet shook her head. It wasn't like her to indulge in daydreams; the three of them co-existed well at the apartment, so why cause herself the unnecessary upheaval of a move? And why should she even consider the possibility of living here?

The kettle boiled on the range fire; the teapot in one hand, the kettle in the other, she called through, 'Tea's made,'

Alan shouted, 'Won't be a minute, just basting the eggs.'

It was an unheard-of event for Jet to sit down to a plateful of bacon and eggs at this time of day. She always breakfasted alone on a pot of black coffee and half a grapefruit, making use of the time to plan her day's work. Now she was eating with relish, enjoying the food, the picnic atmosphere, the desultory conversation.

'You ought to get out in the air today,' Alan told her, squeezing the last cup of tea for them both from the pot. 'It's a lovely morning—put some colour in your cheeks. You're too pale.'

'I stayed to help you with Micah's things,' Jet stated, ignoring his comment on the state of her complexion. 'I suggest we take one room each, go through everything. I daresay most of it will end up on the bonfire.'

'You're bound to be right there.' His eyes crinkled at the corners. 'That thing you're wearing looks like it cost the earth. Haven't you got something scruffier? It's going to be a messy job.'

Alan was wearing old grey flannels and a checked shirt that had seen better days and his get-up, Jet conceded, was far more appropriate than her own.

'What's happening about the furniture?' she asked. The classic grey suit wasn't important; it would dry clean.

Alan shrugged. 'Whoever buys the place can have it. Most of it's only fit for firewood.'

'The dresser isn't bad.' Jet twisted round in her chair to look at the piece in question, deploring the unholy mess on the shelves: battered old saucepans, piles of letters, inches of dust, empty sauce bottles. 'Given a good scrub down and masses of beeswax——' She broke off, smiling into his eyes. 'We'll forget the furniture. As you say, whoever buys the house can have the headache of deciding what to do with it.'

'You're sure you don't want to take advantage of the weather, then?' Alan began to stack plates, clearing the table. 'I didn't ask you to come here to help with the chores.'

'I'd like to help.' Jet left the table, idly crossing to the window, where the sunlit view beckoned, with strange nostalgia. There was a hollow, just over the rise where the thorn trees grew, that was always thick with wild daffodils in the spring. But they'd probably be over now ... She had no wish, in any case, to retread childhood paths ...

A movement half-way down the track caught her eye as she turned to leave the window. A solitary male figure. He had obviously cut across Foundlands land. Even at this distance she could see he was tall, well made, dressed in what appeared to be denim jeans and a dark sweater.

The man didn't hesitate as he began to walk on up the track, his long stride fitting his taller-than-average height. Jet commented idly, not taking her eyes from the stranger,

'Expecting a visitor?'

'Nope.' Alan was re-entering the room, having taken their breakfast things through to the kitchen. 'Someone coming?'

'See for yourself.' Jet moved aside to make room for him at the window and Alan grunted,

'It's the chap who's bought Tipper's Hollow. I told you he's already made noises about wanting to buy this place. Maybe he's coming up to ask me to sell privately— darned if I might just do that, too, if he does ask.'

As the distance between the man on the track and the watchers at the window decreased Jet began to turn away. She might as well clear up in the kitchen, no point in wasting time. Let Alan deal with the crazy man who was so keen to buy this hovel.

But something kept her where she was, watching, and against her better judgment she found her eyes narrowing with something which was more than mere idle curiosity.

Something about the man reminded her of things best left forgotten ... The way the sunlight glinted on his hair, crisp hair cut close to the well-shaped skull, hair the colour of oak leaves in late autumn, of sere bracken, of fox shadows ...

He was close enough to recognise now, and her heart gave a sickening lurch then thudded on. The long amber eyes, the hard, sculpted mouth that was capable of softening to mind-blowing sensuality, the dominant aquiline nose, the naturally dark skin drawn tight over jutting cheekbones ...

Jet couldn't move now, even if she wanted to. And she did want to. She wanted it so much that the flood of adrenalin was painful. Her brain told her to run as she hadn't run for the last six years, to run and hide. Her mind positively hammered out the staccato warnings— Run, for sanity's sake, run! Forget the pride that's made you stand and face every rotten thing life can do. Run! Hide!

But her body, tense as cold steel, wouldn't obey. There was a dull roaring in her ears, a knife thrust of agony deep inside her, a sickening flood of unadulterated hatred coursing through her veins that kept her rooted to the spot, hopelessly trapped by her frenzied emotions as Denzil Fox, the man she had finally and irrevocably cut out of her heart and mind after Tod's death, walked calmly back into her life.

# CHAPTER TWO

HE was as shocked to see her as she had been to see him; there could be no doubt about that. Though shock was too tame a word for the stinging emotion that made every last one of her senses twist and leap in agonised torment.

It had only taken him a split second to recognise her. She saw the almost immediate tightening of his mouth, the hating glitter in his gold eyes. Then Alan was introducing them, unaware that they'd ever met before, insensitive to the taut, animal-like quality of the basic hatred that sparked between them.

Though why Denzil Fox should feel hatred for her was beyond Jet at the moment. 'Call me Denny,' he had once commanded, his voice thick with desire. 'Say "I love you, Denny"; say it, Jet!'

She ignored the hand he reluctantly held towards her as Alan finished his sketchy introduction. She wouldn't touch him. She couldn't touch him! Even the token brushing of hands of supposed strangers on introduction would make her violently, physically sick!

Unmoving, and unmoved by the slight arching of one eyebrow as he acknowledged her refusal to take his hand, by the feral quality of even white teeth exposed in a hard, derisory smile, Jet watched as Alan politely urged him further inside the room, a look of smiling enquiry on his ruddy, honest face.

Outwardly, Jet looked completely in control, her pale, cool features, emphasised by the sleek darkness of her hair, expressionless. Only the ice-hard refraction of light in her vivid blue eyes betrayed the inner screaming of every nerve end.

What was he doing here? Why hang around this place, a haunting shade from the past who ought to be cringing in shame for what he had done instead of holding himself with arrogance, his poise sickening her as he asked,

'I expect you've a fair idea of why I'm here, Taylor? Is there somewhere we could talk in private?'

Jet only just managed to control the angry hiss of indrawn breath his insulting words provoked, and her fighting spirit surged back, stronger than ever for its brief absence. She felt only hatred and contempt for the man whose fox-shadow head was held high, whose easy stance, his back turned on her, was consciously dismissive.

Instinctively, as she had known he would, Alan glanced uneasily towards her, his light eyes questioning. Behind Denny's back Jet gave a slow shake of her head, a slight warning frown. Denny Fox would find he couldn't dismiss her so easily. He was no longer dealing with a half-wild waif—trusting, gullible and painfully ignorant. He had Jet Luellyn to contend with. Mature, hard as bright steel and just about as sharp—Jet Luellyn, alias Roger Blye, whose earning capacity would leave him speechless when he recalled the little ignoramus who had once hung, enchanted and impressed, on his every clever, lying word.

Alan cleared his throat, his feet solidly apart.

'You can say what you've come to say in front of Jet. We've no secrets.'

No secrets? When the biggest secret in her life was standing here, right between them, Jet thought, fighting back crazy laughter as Denny turned slowly, his eyes insulting as they swept the slender length of her. But his insolent scrutiny did not reach her eyes, and he missed the burning fury that blazed in the sapphire depths before being quickly, expertly battened down, shuttered by the aloof appearance of complete self-control which held an underlying hint of boredom.

'It's about Foundlands,' Denny said, turning to Alan, his voice smooth. 'Though I daresay you'd guessed that much. I'd like you, if you would, to agree to a private sale. I'm prepared to offer well over the reserve.'

'Cancel the auction? The thought had crossed my mind.' Alan was at ease again, interested in what was being said. 'It beats me why you want it, though.'

'Let's say it's an obsession of mine.' Even though his back was excludingly turned on her, Jet could sense the charm of his smile as he went on, explaining easily, 'I find I can't be here on the day fixed for the sale, which means I'd either have to leave my bid or get someone to sit in for me. The other alternative is for us to make a private deal. Shall we talk business, Taylor?'

Confidence oozed from him, Jet noted savagely. The way he held his head, the easy, graceful set of his wide shoulders, the very way he stood his piece of ground, indicated a man who was used to getting his own way, always, and to hell with the opposition.

And the thought of him, of all people, owning Foundlands, having access to the place that had been part of her life—the only part for twelve long years—revolted her. He had no right here, no right beneath the roof that had sheltered the half-wild lonely child she had once been. It implied an intimacy that sickened her. And Jet intended to make sure he never had that right.

Her beautiful, clear voice was cool and steady, an echo of the cold core of inner strength she could call on at will, as she said smoothly, finding and holding Alan's eyes, 'You're a little too late, Mr Fox. What a frightful shame!' She saw how he stiffened at her injection of sarcasm and she continued unhurriedly, enjoying the feeling that she was now fighting him on her own terms, with her own weapons. 'I am buying Foundlands. Alan and I have already agreed our price. So sorry you've wasted your time. Good day to you.'

She didn't wait to see his reaction. She wasn't interested in his reaction. She had deprived him of something he wanted, and that was enough. Alan would never agree to sell Foundlands to anyone else if he knew she wanted it, and she could match any price Denny Fox could offer.

Jet left the room with a serenity that astounded herself, and she banished the fit of weak trembling that gripped her as soon as she'd closed the kitchen door by the simple expedient of getting on with the washing up.

A few minutes later Alan was in the room with her, his features showing a mixture of amusement and perplexity. 'Have you gone crazy, or do you really want this dump?'

'Has he gone?'

'Yes. Right now I'd say he's a very angry man. What are you up to, Jet?' Alan grabbed a tea towel and began to wipe the dishes she was stacking on the draining board. Jet flicked him a sideways look that told him nothing.

'Why should I be up to anything?' she parried, the purity of her cool profile betraying nothing of the stinging elation she felt at having put Denny Fox firmly in his place. As far as she was concerned his place was under her heel. 'I suddenly realised I didn't want Foundlands to go out of the family,' she lied. 'I'm sorry I had to spring it on you like that, but I could see you were on the point of making a deal with Fox, so I thought I'd better speak up quickly. You don't mind, do you?'

She knew he didn't mind; she had taken that for

granted. All the same, her conscience twinged uneasily as he followed her into the other room, the damp tea towel still dangling from his fingers.

'Hell, no! I'll be happy to have you living nearby. I'll be able to keep an eye on you!'

He seemed delighted by the prospect, and Jet, her conscience pricking more deeply now, remembering the time when he'd said he loved her, and uneasy because he'd never married in all the years since she'd turned him down, said hurriedly, 'Maybe you should go ahead with the auction in any case. Fox and I can fight it out.' The idea appealed to her; whatever sum he went to, she'd better it—even if she had to sell everything she owned to do it. It went as deep as that for her. 'You'd get a better price that way,' she added seriously.

'You can forget that!' Alan's eyes were amused. 'Mr Fox asked me if what you'd said was true. I told him yes, I'd agreed to sell to you. He left looking as if he'd like to murder both of us.'

'Good. Let's get down to brass tacks.'

Jet accepted his decision not to let the house go to auction. He was a mature adult and she respected his intelligence and he was, she knew, as forthright as she was herself when it came to business dealings. So she was unprepared for his uncomfortable, 'I can't take your money, Jet. Good God—the place should have been left to you by rights. I said that as soon as I knew he'd left it to me, and I've been thinking it ever since.'

She saw the stubborn set of his mouth, the trace of anxiety in his eyes. 'If you take that attitude I'm backing out.' Her mouth firmed decisively. 'I won't ever come near the place again. What have you set the reserve at? If you don't tell me I can soon find out.'

'Forty-five thousand,' he told her edgily, his shoulders

hunched as he turned to stare into the fire burning in the range.

'Then shall we settle on fifty-five? Fox would have gone that much higher at least. So if anything, I'm doing you down, not the other way around,' she said more softly as she saw the beginnings of anger in his normally placid grey eyes. No man likes having his altruism thrown back in his face. 'Are you doing so well you can afford to throw fifty-five thousand away?'

Jet acknowledged his wry shrug with her seldom seen but heartwarming grin. 'Thanks to Roger Blye I won't notice too much of a dent in my bank balance,' she said, making a joke of it. 'And if you're cussed enough to feel bad about taking my money then you can salve your pride, or whatever it is that's bugging you, by sticking around long enough to help me get the builders organised. I shan't want to hang around for months before I move in. Now, buddy, we've got a lot of phoning to do.'

She reached for the leather shoulder bag she'd left hitched over the back of a chair and extracted a slim Morocco-bound notebook, flicking through to find the telephone numbers she needed, ignoring his half-grumbled comment, 'For a girl who looks as if a stiff wind would blow her over, you act remarkably like a steamroller, Jet!'

The rest of the day passed swiftly. They used the phone in turn. Alan broke the news to the estate agent acting on his behalf and contacted two local building firms, asking them to send someone out to give estimates for the necessary repair work. They phoned their respective solicitors and Jet arranged for the London apartment to be sub-let, fully furnished, and asked Barbie to notify her agent and publishers of her imminent change of address.

Barbie was more intrigued than thrown by her

employer's sudden decision to move, and when Jet told her, 'I'll leave everything that end to you. I'll stay up here until the alterations are well under way—I want this place to be habitable by the end of May,' all Barbie said was, 'Good. Ben and I will look forward to it. And if anything requires your signature I'll send it on; otherwise, I'll handle everything as usual.'

Jet signed everything to do with the professional side of her life using her pen-name, and Barbie, as her secretary, dealt with all phone calls from her agent, her publishers, or people from the media who wanted an interview with the reclusive but highly succesful author, Roger Blye.

Jet was a very private person, and no one except Barbie and Alan knew that Roger Blye was a woman. She felt that the essentially male-orientated books would lose something if it were generally known that their author was female. She also believed that an author's identity and personality had nothing to do with the product that was offered for public consumption on book shelves and film screens.

'Let's call it a day.' Alan came downstairs with an armful of Micah's better garments—those he'd deemed fit for the next village jumble sale.

The light was beginning to fade from the sky and Jet had spent most of the afternoon and evening turning out the kitchen, so she was ready to agree to his suggestion. But she shook her head doubtfully when he suggested a meal at the village pub.

'As a celebration,' he offered. 'And I don't know about you, but I don't much feel like cooking after the hard graft we've put in today.'

'There's one of your mother's home made veal and ham pies in the fridge,' Jet pointed out, dropping an unsavoury-looking frying pan on to the rest of the junk in the tea chest Alan had provided for the rubbish. 'I honestly don't feel like going out. All I want is a hot bath.'

Her hair was coming adrift and if her face was as filthy as her hands and her erstwhile immaculate trouser suit, then it would take a lot of effort, not to mention soap and hot water, to achieve her normal sophisticated, smoothly groomed exterior.

'I'll make a salad to go with the pie and we can both relax in comfort instead of having to doll ourselves up to go out.'

As always, going way back to the summer holidays when they'd been children together, Alan was willing to fall in with her plans, finding them, somehow, more to his taste than those he'd thought up himself.

'You could be right.' He pulled a face at his own disreputable clothes. 'It'll take me a month of Sundays to get clean and presentable again.'

He had finally come to terms with his dislike of taking her money for what he honestly thought should have been hers all along, and he wasn't going to let what he now saw as an occasion for celebration slip by unmarked.

'I'll get the worst of the grime off then slip down to the pub for a couple of bottles of wine.'

Ten minutes later, freshly shaved and wearing clean but well-worn denim jeans and jacket, Alan went out to the Land Rover and Jet walked upstairs to the bathroom he'd just vacated.

Now that the need for any real mental or physical activity was over her keen, restless mind focused sharply on the events of that morning. It had been an easy matter to shut Denny Fox out of her mind while she had been involved in making the arrangements for buying Foundlands and disposing of the lease on her home in London. She was always able to concentrate on the job in hand to the exclusion of all extraneous matter. And there was no matter more extraneous to her way of thinking than Denzil Fox.

Similarly, with the more physical chore of cleaning out the disgusting kitchen, getting rid of the dirt and unlovely clutter of years, she had been able to keep her mind solely on that.

Now, lying back in the hot sudsy water, Denny intruded, slamming his way back into a mind that had successfully relegated him to non-existence years ago.

Seeing him again, when she hadn't allowed herself to think of him in years, had opened a floodgate of hurtful memories. She had to banish them for a second time. If she didn't she would go insane!

Springing out of the chipped bath, she wrapped a threadbare towel, the only clean one she'd been able to find, around her tautly slender body, and went to the handbasin to wash her hair.

Fiercely concentrating on every economical movement, to the complete exclusion of every other thought, she washed and rinsed her hair, dragging a comb punishingly through its tangled length before going to her room and huddling into a dark blue housecoat in fine pure wool and cinching the tie belt narrowly around her waist.

Devoid of make-up, her heavy shoulder-length hair still damp but drying in soft tendrils around her face, she looked younger than her twenty-four years. Her mirror image appeared more like the uncontrolled adolescent she had been in the long hot summer of her eighteenth year.

Jet shoved that thought away with a brutality that might have hurt if she hadn't been beyond hurting any more. That half-wild girl with the mane of glossy, storm-dark hair—the girl who had craved love with all the intensity of an emotional nature long denied any affection at all, was dead. Long gone and quite quite dead, as far as Jet was concerned.

Pushing her feet into comfortable mules, she left the room quickly and hurried down the twisting, ill-lit stairs, determinedly intent on the things she had to do: slice the pie, wash the salad, set the table. Only by mentally seeing herself perform the mundane chores could she block unwanted thoughts.

It was dark inside the house now. Jet flicked the light on in the small hallway for Alan's benefit then turned to the kitchen, looking back as a sharp rapping drew her attention to the front door.

Without thinking—and later she was to curse herself for not thinking—she swung round again, automatically taking the tarnished brass handle and opening the door.

He almost filled the door frame, his shadowed figure silhouetted starkly against the hazy amethyst of the evening sky. His features were indistinct, the strong bones and sharp planes a colour wash in tones of grey.

For Jet, for one fleeting moment, she was seeing again the face of the man who had been her whole world. The lover of her heart and mind and body, the mystical prince of her young, romantic imaginings, the one she had waited for all her life, the delight and wonder of her soul.

And for that one fleeting moment her heart thudded again to the wild sweet music of worshipping, unthinking love, the song in a strange land that had seduced her senses until there was nothing left to be done but submit her entire being to his will and follow the strange music of the heart, wherever it led.

The moment passed, killed stone dead by her hard-won sense of survival. The man standing in her doorway was no mystical lover whose very smile could tame the wildest spirit, whose softly voiced words could seduce the soul from the body, whose beautiful yet strong hands could work unbelievable magic.

He was a shallow-minded liar and cheat, an abomin-
ation. And she hated and despised him with the passion
with which she had once loved him.

Her reaction was swift, but not as swift as his. A strong
arm, powered by lithely muscular shoulders, slammed
out to hold the door as she attempted to shut it in his face.
Without speaking, he pushed past her into the hall.
Under the overhead light she could see that he'd changed
little in six years. The lines of his face were harder, more
sternly drawn, and his eyes were colder. But his vital
attraction had not blurred; his lean body was just as
strong and fit as it had ever been.

Jet closed her eyes briefly at the unwanted memory of
how that hard body had felt beneath her hands—hands
that had been shy at first, unsure. Then, later, wanting,
demanding, craving the love she needed, finding that
love in his answering passion—or so she in her foolish
naïveté had believed.

'It's been a long time, Jet. But I knew if I waited I'd run
across you again.'

The cutting edge of his voice brought her eyes winging
open. They were wide, liquid jewels, still hazed from the
intimacy of that unwanted but unstoppable memory of
how his body had felt.

He stepped back, leaning against the newel post, his
attitude proprietorial, as if he had every right in the
world to be where he was. His amber eyes, curiously
expressionless, raked slowly over her.

Her instinct was to look away, to pull the revealing
deep V of her robe more closely together. But she
automatically repudiated the defensive path; her eyes
didn't waver from his face and her hands remained,
tightly clenched, at her sides.

'Get the hell out of here!' Jet's salvation lay in anger

and it rose now, a quick, strangely exciting surge of hating that whipped through her veins like the lick of savage fire it was, splashing her high cheek bones with vivid colour, darkening her eyes to midnight ice.

'You've grown more beautiful,' was his only comment. It wasn't a compliment, more a bitter disparagement. There was a dent of derision at one side of his mouth as he stated, 'That thing you're wearing didn't come from a jumble sale, and the car you drive wasn't picked up for next to nothing in a breaker's yard. You've done nicely for yourself—congratulations. For a half-tamed scrubber with hardly a rag to her back, you've done very nicely indeed.'

The long amber eyes dropped to her ringless left hand then slammed back to her face, hardening perceptibly.

'You've never married? No, I didn't expect you would have done—not until your looks start to go off. There are better pickings for a woman like you if she's unencumbered.'

She drew in a long silent breath, her delicate nostrils flaring as she fought against the unbelievable pain, the power he had to hurt her again . . . and again.

'I don't know what you're doing here,' she rasped, her voice caught by the constriction in her throat, 'but I want you out.'

'Yes, I daresay you do. But who's going to do it? You?'

Jet was tall for a girl and harboured enough inner tension to give her a tensile strength far beyond what might have been expected from her slender bone structure. But he topped her by a head and, beyond his powerful build, he'd acquired a toughness, an aura of menace that left her in no doubt that he wouldn't hesitate to use that strength on her if she attempted to make him leave.

'And don't try to tell me that you'll get your boy-friend

to throw me out,' he clipped insultingly. 'He'd need a private army with him to do that. Besides, I saw him drive down in the direction of the village.'

His words slid through her chaotic thoughts and her head snapped up high, her lips curling with disgust as one more reason why she should despise him presented itself.

'How typically cowardly. You wouldn't have dared come here and say the things you've said had Alan been here.'

Her icy hauteur was incomparable, her words calculated to wound. Denzil Fox pushed himself away from the newel post, his anger under precarious control.

'Damn you for a two-timing whore, Jet Luellyn! Damn your poisonous tongue!'

His anger had left him visibly shaken, his face white, pulled tight with the rage he was having trouble confining. His voice was thick with it as he walked right up to her, his eyes burning holes in the ashen fury of his face.

'I don't give a pig's eye for lover-boy! I came when I knew he was out of the way because what I have to say to you is private. It's private and it's sick—like every other thing there's ever been between us.'

Jet stood her ground, her expression carefully controlled. But she was shaken by his emotion. His loathing for her seemed a tangible thing, something that reached out and enveloped them both in a tight world of shared need. A need for the hatred to continue, to be fuelled and refuelled until it consumed them both. Any other emotion between them would be unthinkable, because of what had gone before.

His face was calmer now, colour coming back, his voice quieter as he said, 'You and lover-boy took me for a ride today. I don't blame him, poor sucker. He would have been prepared to sell this place to me until you

slipped your loaded oar in. You and he hadn't settled on
any sale until I walked through that door. One word from
you and the poor, besotted fool was eating out of your
hands. Did he hand over the deeds, all tied up with
ribbon, Jet? And what's he getting in return? A few more
nights of bliss until you decide it's time to give him the
old heave-ho?'

She stared at him disbelievingly, her face drawn,
looking older with the effort it took to control the urge to
scratch and kick and bite—to give rein to her need to hit
and hurt. She didn't trust herself to speak, but her blazing
eyes were willing him to drop dead.

'You're welcome to the place, Jet,' he told her flatly.
Then, moving closer so that she could feel his body heat,
his voice thickening, he went on, 'That's twice you've
taken me for a sucker. No one gets away with that once,
let alone twice. I've waited for years to make you pay for
the first time. Years, Jet. Years of coming back here
whenever I could make the time, years of waiting. I knew
you'd show up here sooner or later. I knew I'd eventually
get the chance to make you pay for that first time.'

He moved away, going towards the door, and there
was a stark note of nemesis in his voice as he said,
'There's a double dose of retribution due to you now.
Sleep well, my lovely Jet.'

## CHAPTER THREE

IT was another lovely morning. Jet looked round the transformed sitting-room at Foundlands, her eyes softening. Already it felt like home, and it had never felt remotely home-like when she'd lived here with Micah.

The cream-washed walls made an easy background for the antique cottage furniture that now took the place of her uncle's shabby bits and pieces. But the dresser had been restored and now carried her newly acquired blue Delftware. She and Alan had found the rest of the furniture for the farmhouse by scouring local antique shops and haunting sale rooms.

Strange that she should at last want to put roots down—and here, of all places!

The sound of an engine, carefully crawling up the track, broke into her pleasant musings. Barbie was back. Jet had sold the BMW, substituting a roomy estate car that was more suitable for everyday use in the sticks. She had realised ruefully that by purchasing the prestigious car she had been trying to convince herself that the girl who had grown up having nothing could at last afford anything she wanted.

'Hi, there!' Barbie breezed through the room, heading for the kitchen with a carton of groceries. She had her son Ben in tow, his auburn curls unnaturally slicked down, the jeans and T-shirt he'd lived in since he and his mother had joined Jet at Foundlands ten days ago replaced by short blue trousers and a neat white shirt—a concession to his visit that morning to the local school's headmistress.

'What a glorious day!' Barbie carolled from the kitchen. 'As I said to myself just now, all this, and heaven, too!' She poked her head round the kitchen door, grinning, her pert face surrounded by red-gold curls. 'And I do mean heaven—in the shape of the most fantastic-looking guy I've seen in years! He's dropping by for coffee—is that okay with you? Oh, and Miss Lovatt from the primary says Ben can start on Monday. She say's it'll give him a chance to get to know his way around, make friends and so on, before he's five and can start in earnest in the autumn. Hey, you—drop it!'

Barbie twirled round, taking a packet of chocolate-covered biscuits from Ben's clutching hands and dropping them back in the carton.

'Just as well all mums are born with eyes in the backs of their heads!' She rumpled Ben's hair affectionately then patted his small backside. 'You can have your biscuits and juice when you've changed into your play gear. Scoot!'

Ben scooted, his sturdy legs carrying him towards the stairs, the look on his face proclaiming that at almost five he knew his own mind but could weigh up the pros and cons and saw that the best way to what he most wanted at the moment—chocolate biscuits and a few flights on the swing Alan had fixed to one of the trees—was to follow his mother's instructions.

Jet watched him leave the room, her eyes dead. Tod, her own baby, would have been about Ben's age, had he lived.

Her movements were uncharacteristically slow as she lifted a pot plant out of the direct sunlight and carried it to a shadier part of the room. She knew she should be doing something about getting down to some serious work, but felt unable to confine herself right now to the small study she'd created from the room where Micah had kept a clutter of veterinary supplies and feed supplements. Her typewriter was waiting, the pages and pages of research notes—everything she needed to make a start on her new book.

'. . . and he said he'd come at about eleven. Now, are you quite sure you don't mind?'

Jet had to force herself to take some notice of the one-sided conversation coming from the kitchen where Barbie was stowing groceries. She glanced at her watch. Five-to. Just the prod she needed, she supposed without much enthusiasm, to get her to her desk. She didn't particularly want to meet Barbie's 'Heavenly Man'!

'Of course. Invite who you like—you know that.' Jet left the tantalising sunlit view afforded by the sparkling clean window hung with attractive print curtains. 'Who is this guy, anyway?'

'Denzil Fox.'

Barbie came out of the kitchen, tucking her sleeveless blouse more securely into the waistband of her jeans, patting at her curvaceous hips as if the discontented action would magic away a few unwanted pounds.

'I met him outside the village store—he stopped Ben from running under the wheels of a van, actually. We got talking after I'd stopped having hysterics and it turned out we were neighbours. So I did the neighbourly thing and invited him up for coffee. After all,' her brown eyes sobered, 'he did save Ben from a very nasty accident. Besides,' she shrugged, looking incorrigible again, 'he's a real dish! You've no idea!'

Jet had a very good idea. She hadn't taken in too much of what Barbie had been saying; she'd been too shocked by the sound of that name.

Blood thudded thickly through her veins and her legs felt too heavy to move. But yes, Denny Fox was quite a dish—if one didn't take the trouble to look behind the attractive façade to find the cheating soul beneath!

She hadn't seen him since the night he'd walked in here and lashed her with his tongue. But he had been present in her thoughts, there was no getting away from that. No matter how hard she'd tried to push him away, he'd been there.

Daytimes hadn't been so bad. She had had the demanding job of keeping the builders up to scratch, clearing up after them, finding decorators willing to go to work immediately, buying furnishings.

But every night as she had tried to sleep he'd been right there in her head, an agonising reminder of things best left forgotten.

'Jet—are you all right? You've gone horribly pale.'

Jet pulled herself together. She had to get out of the house before Denny arrived. She had to get out of here!

'I'm fine. I've got a bit of a headache, that's all. I think I'll go out and get some air.'

She smiled down into Barbie's face, seeing the enquiring frown smooth out, then hot colour flooded her cheeks as the well-remembered voice called out from the hall, 'Anybody home?'

It couldn't be happening, Jet thought, suddenly nauseous. Pressing fingertips to her temples, she knew she had to face him now. It was one thing to run before he arrived, manufacturing excuses for Barbie's consumption, but quite another to let him know he'd driven her out of her own home. And he would know.

Barbie preceded him into the room, her cheeks pink. Taking in his superb athlete's body, dressed in narrow whipcord pants and a skin-hugging sage green T-shirt, Jet could see why. The charm of his smile was very much in evidence, too, as he asked, 'Over the shakes now, Barbie?'

'Oh, yes.' She sounded breathless, her big eyes shining

into his. 'But I'll never forget what it felt like to see Ben run out into the road like that. If you hadn't been there——'

'He wouldn't have come to much harm,' Denny reassured softly, his eyes warm. 'Truly. The van was travelling very slowly. The driver would have been able to stop in time.'

'Even so——' Barbie's soft mouth took on a firm line. She was determined not to be done out of giving gratitude. 'Even so, it was a shock, and I'll never forget what you did. Oh!' Her mouth dropped open. 'I was forgetting! This is my employer, Jet——'

'We've met.' Denny cut into Barbie's belated introductions, and it was as if another man stared out of the eyes that had so recently been filled with warmth and reassurance. A ruthless, unforgiving man with hatred in his heart. He dragged a long, insulting look over her body, and Jet's stomach clenched in a sickening knot.

At least she looked the part of an unemotional professional woman, she assured herself. Hair neatly coiled, plain gold stud earrings, tailored dark grey cotton skirt, severe pale grey shirt. All she had to do was act the part, show him he couldn't get to her, not any more.

Cutting through Barbie's twittered exhortations for him to sit down and make himself comfortable while she fixed the coffee, Jet made her features expressionless, her clear, lovely voice quite calm, and said, 'I'll make coffee, Barbie. You entertain your guest.'

She'd drink a cup of coffee then make her excuses and go to her study. That way it wouldn't look as if he had driven her away. Ben had come downstairs by the time Jet carried the tray through. The three of them were sitting on the sofa under the window, Ben looking quite at home leaning against Denny's knees, Barbie chattering nineteen to the dozen, looking animated.

Poised in the doorway, Jet felt like screaming and could barely raise a nod of thanks when Barbie jumped up to take the tray from her then scurried out to the kitchen to fetch juice and biscuits for Ben.

Denny gently put the child aside. 'Run and help your mother, Ben.' He stood up slowly, gracefully, like a cat. 'Happy in your new home, Jet?' he asked smoothly, his question like a threat.

'Why did you come?' Her voice was cold, calculatedly so. Her eyes were colder.

'I was invited.'

'Not by me. You're not welcome here.'

'I know that. Care to tell your delightful secretary exactly why?'

Amber eyes held biting scorn, and Jet knew that he knew she'd have to be on her last gasp, defeated and beaten, before she told anyone what a gullible idiot she'd once been.

'Right, let's have that coffee, folks!' Barbie bounced back in again, closely followed by Ben, who drank his juice in one long swallow then ran out of the room and up the stairs.

Denny and Jet broke eye contact slowly, as if something unknown, frightening, held them together. He returned to the sofa, accepting the cup Barbie held out, giving a warm smile to the girl who was clearly growing more smitten by the second.

Jet took her cup to a chair by the empty fireplace, pity for Barbie rising in a stinging tide. She didn't know what she was letting herself in for if she allowed herself to be taken in by his spurious charm.

As far as Jet knew—and she knew a great deal about the girl who had not only been her secretary for the past two years but was probably the nearest thing to a friend she'd ever had—Barbie hadn't looked at a man since her

young husband had been killed in a climbing accident a
few days before Ben's birth.

But she was looking now.

Watching them, close together on the sofa, Jet felt
physically sick. The coffee cooling in her cup would
choke her if she tried to drink it. Denny was smiling at
Barbie's non-stop chatter, his fox-shadow head almost
touching her much redder curls, his hard mouth taking
on a sensual curve that twisted a knife deep inside her.

Just watching him put on the charm, act as if no other
woman existed but Barbie, made Jet ill. Why had the
devious devil accepted that invitation for coffee? Why,
when he knew Jet would rather let a marauding tiger
through the door?

Sitting primly on her own, excluded by the others, for
all the world like an unwanted and forgotten visitor
rather than mistress in her own home, Jet knew why he'd
come. He had come because he had known it would
throw her. Even if he hadn't met Barbie in such dramatic
circumstances, he would have found a way to place her in
the frustrating position of having to accept him under her
roof as her secretary's guest.

Watching carefully from beneath long dark lashes, Jet
wondered for the thousandth time just why he hated her.
She had thought, when he'd walked back into her life,
that she was capable of a hatred so deep it was
unfathomable. But set beside his obvious loathing for
her, hers was kindergarten stuff. It puzzled her, and if
she were honest, frightened her silly.

She had never done a thing to hurt or harm him. All
she had done was worship him with the blind,
unthinking adoration of one who had been starved of
love for a long, long time.

Something Barbie said, her voice pitched too low for
Jet to hear clearly, made Denny throw back his head and

laugh aloud, his strong throat rippling. Barbie's eyes dropped, her smile flustered and pleased, and Ben came into the room with his latest Meccano creation, the delights of the swing forgotten in his desire to impress the visitor.

As the child climbed on the sofa Denny pulled him into the curve of his arm, bending to admire the toy held out for his inspection.

Jet jerked to her feet, pain filling her. Seeing the man and the child together, sensing the growth of an affectionate bond, couldn't be borne.

Her control slipping under the weight of the indescribable pain that came out of nowhere, she walked stiffly from the room. She could feel his eyes boring into her back—almost see the coldly triumphant look in his knowing amber eyes.

Jet sat at her desk, shuffling papers. She had placed it so that her back was to the window, avoiding the distraction of the view up to Crow's Top. Until recently the strength of her will, her determination to succeed and carry on succeeding, would have admitted no distraction whatsoever.

But nowadays her mind seemed to be anywhere but where she wanted it to be: on Denny Fox, mostly. It was terrifying to discover how easily he could destroy the controlled, hard person she had forced herself to become. But then he was a destroyer.

She closed her eyes, pale lids descending to hide the haunted look in their vivid blue depths as she forced herself to concentrate. She took several deep, slow breaths, deliberately blocking him and the painful memories he evoked out of her mind. She would not let those memories come through. She couldn't cope with them. It was enough that his reappearance in her life was

relentlessly prodding them to the front of her mind. She
mustn't let them surface. She mustn't let him win!

After a few minutes her breathing became more
natural and she rolled a sheet of paper into the typewriter
and tapped out 'Chapter One'. Concentrating steadily
now, she managed two paragraphs, only to have the flow
broken before it had really started by the sound of
Barbie's light laughter, Denny's answering deeper tones,
drifting back from the hall at the front of the house.

Jet's fingers froze, hovering over the keys, then lifted
to her face, pressing her temples. Damn him for his
pernicious intrusion! He was breaking her up, killing her
peace of mind. Was this what he had planned when he'd
spoken of retribution?

She knew it was, and it had nothing to do with her
having bested him over the sale of this house. It went far
deeper than that. She had seen the hatred in his eyes the
moment he'd recognised her. And he'd talked of waiting
for her, of knowing she would come back here some time,
of planning his revenge for that first time.

What first time, for God's sake? Jet groaned, unable to
make any sense of it. She hadn't done one thing to hurt
him; she had only loved him. It was she who should be
seeking retribution!

Jet heard Barbie walk back through the hall, saying
something to Ben who piped a shrill protest. Knowing
she couldn't pretend to work through the long warm
afternoon, not while her mind was in such confusion, and
knowing she couldn't listen to Barbie's chatter which
would, she guessed, be centred on Denny Fox and his
attractions, Jet left the room, calling through to the
kitchen, 'Don't make lunch for me, I'm going out for
some air.'

She felt calmer outside. The air was full of birdsong,

heavy with the scent of hedge parsley which drifted like a low white cloud on the verge of the track. Jet breathed deeply as she strode out across the near meadow, her long-legged stride carrying her gracefully over the springy grass.

She kept to the lower-lying land, the slim cut of her tailored skirt precluding the rougher going over the high places where she had roamed at will in her childhood. Often, as she had grown older and more uneasy with her home life and the blows and curses of the uncle who resented her, she stayed out until dawn, spending the short warm summer nights stretched out on the heather, watching the stars and dreaming dreams.

There had been more brutality, more obscene words when, as often as not, he'd caught her creeping back into the house. But by then she had learned to endure them, accept them as an inevitable part of her life with the sour-tempered elderly man who begrudged her every mouthful of food she ate, refused to let her bring her school friends home or to visit their homes in the village.

Not that there had been many school friends, she recalled, stopping to lean against the gate at the far end of the meadow. Her peers had regarded her as an oddity, someone to be laughed at and teased rather than befriended. She'd been a wild-haired child with wide, restless, seeking eyes, dressed in ill-fitting hand-me-downs.

And she hadn't been at school much, either. At least not after she'd grown big enough to help Micah around the farm. And so she had found escape in the hills, running wild, keeping away as much as she could from the bitter old man, finding her happiness in simple things: the clear running waters of a hill stream, the tiny flowers and wild creatures who shared her lonely wanderings, the soaring splendour of the vast hilly tracts of rock and whin and bogland where the soft winds blew, sweet with the tang of pine and heather and sun-warmed grass . . .

Jet roused herself, opened the gate and walked through, closing it carefully behind her. A wry smile tugged her mouth. It would have been unheard of for her to open a gate in the old days; she would simply have vaulted over! She would have to buy more suitable gear if she meant to do much walking in future.

Taking an oblique line, she followed the incline of the steep bank stretching before her, making for the hazel trees which bordered the stream. She was easier now in her mind, able to think more rationally.

Buying Foundlands, coming to live here, was probably the least sensible thing she could have done. She had known Denny used Tipper's Hollow as an occasional weekend home. So buying Foundlands, merely to let him know he couldn't always get what he wanted, had been a bad mistake. Since Tod had died she hadn't allowed herself to make mistakes. But Denny Fox and her highly emotional response to seeing him again had forced her into this one.

Feeling the breeze tug at her hair, she automatically fixed a wandering strand back in place, then bent her head to pass beneath the low-growing branches of the hazels. It was cool beneath the trees, the murmur of the stream soothing, conducive to logical thought.

Her work was the most important part of her life now, and would be for as far ahead in the future as she cared to look. So, if she found she couldn't concentrate because of the bad feelings Denny roused in her, couldn't come to terms with the possibility of him popping in and out of her life like a sinister Jack-in-the-box, then she'd have to sell up and move. It really was as simple as that.

Basically unwilling to allow him to emerge the victor in

what she now saw would be a bitter, ongoing battle of wills, but reassured because there was a way out after all, albeit a cowardly one, she walked on, enjoying the green shade afforded by the leafy canopy overhead. But she stopped short, shaken, when she came up to a low fence with a strip of clipped lawn beyond.

Of course—it was the back of Tipper's Hollow! How could she have been so stupid as to have taken her walk in this direction! And why hadn't she remembered Alan saying that Denny had bought the strip of land along the stream bank? Or did her body follow instincts her mind refused to tolerate!

Jet turned quickly, her heart constricting then racing on, making her breath come in fast, fluttering rhythm, her legs feel unsteady as if they would give way under her at any moment.

As she emerged from the trees at last she could hear following footsteps, the tell-tale rustle of last year's dry leaves, the cracking of twigs. The sunlight striking through the thin fabric of her shirt felt unbearably hot. Perspiration suddenly dewed her face and trickled edgily down the cleft between her breasts. She didn't need to be told that the man who stalked her beneath the trees was Denny Fox. She knew.

He caught up with her before she could take to her heels and run. His hand grasped her shoulder, pressing the slender bones, forcing her to face him. And then, staring up as if mesmerised into the handsome face, seeing the lurking dislike in his golden eyes suddenly flare into bitterness, she was glad she hadn't had time to do anything so undignified and revealing as run from him.

'Are you following me?' Her eyes met his unwaveringly, sapphire holding amber with matched dislike as she commanded, 'Get your hands off me!'

Trying to twist away from his hold on her without showing the panic that was churning inside her, she felt his hard fingers bite more deeply, bone on bone. There was a pulse beating erratically at the base of his throat and his jawline was hard with inner tension.

Her eyes slid away as her own body tensed up until she thought the pulling of it would tear her physically apart.

'You are on my land.' The words were like the breaking of ice, coming from lips curved down in contempt, the character lines on either side of his mouth running deep. 'And to echo your phrase of earlier, you're not welcome.'

Her heart was fluttering like a caged wild bird, but it didn't show as her cool pure features permitted a slight, quelling smile. Not for the world would she let him know just how he affected her hard-won peace of mind.

'How too, too frightful of me!' Her voice was a deliberate parody of sophisticated disdain. 'I shall have to be more careful where I put my feet in future. One can pick up such unspeakable things on one's travels—don't you agree, Mr Fox?'

He released her then, pushing his hands deep in the pockets of his snug-fitting trousers as if to prevent himself from strangling her there and then.

Conscious of a victory, however slight, yet full of a strange, sharp hurting in spite of it, she turned as coolly as she could to go, unable to resist a parting shot,

'So sorry to have come near you. As you can imagine, it wasn't intentional. I'll make sure it doesn't happen again.'

She hadn't moved two paces before his hands were on her arms, wrenching her round. Stumbling, she fell against him, her breath coming shallow and fast as he bit out savagely,

'You little bitch!'

The face above her was dark with fury, his white teeth showing in a snarl as his mouth descended on hers, forcing her lips back against her teeth, forcing them apart. The pressure of his mouth increased, castigating, bruising, his hand going to the back of her head, scattering pins until her hair fell around her in a dusky cloud, imprisoned by his twining fingers.

His other hand went to her back, pulling her closer so that she could feel the hard muscles of his thighs straining against her, feel the heat of his body burning into her.

Jet moaned, fighting him, fighting the shaming explosion of need, the heated sensation that flooded her, threatening to drown her in its violent spate.

The moaning in her throat became a whimper as she struggled to get free of his punishing embrace, fought to hold back the memory of other kisses that had been light years away from this hating assault.

Suddenly, as if sickened by the deadly game he had instigated, he thrust her roughly aside, his features contorted in a self-derisory mask as she fell to the ground, sprawling on the sun-warmed grass like a broken doll.

He stood over her briefly, legs planted apart, his breathing ragged, sweat running in rivulets down his corded neck.

He watched her from narrowed eyes and contempt lifted a corner of his mouth as he turned and strode away.

# CHAPTER FOUR

HER breath coming in painful spasms, Jet leaned weakly against the outcrop of rock, then sank slowly to the short turf at its base, her knees folded under her.

She hadn't stopped running since she'd picked herself up from where Denny had thrown her, and Crow's Top was as high as she could go. Gingerly, she put a hand to her mouth, her fingers trembling against the soft bruised lips he had taken so savagely. Her deep blue eyes, wide with shock, stared unseeingly out over the range of tumbled hills, the spire of the village church distantly visible in one of the green-flanked folds.

That embrace, even though the emotive force behind it had been hatred, had brought memories to her mind, screaming to be acknowledged. She had tried to run from them, as if to leave them physically behind, but they were right here with her still, pounding inside her head, undeniable, demanding release.

Her head dropped forward on her long slim neck, her dark hair wildly tangled, adrift from the careful propriety of pins. Her knees and shins were aching from the cuts and bruises she had collected on her unthinking scramble upwards, her clothes ruined beyond redemption. But she was aware of none of this as tension slipped away into defeat and the memories she'd fought against for so long came crowding back as she re-lived the day that had marked her eighteenth birthday . . .

She woke very early, rolling on to her back and staring up at the cracked ceiling. Eighteen years old today! Jet jackknifed out of bed, filled with the edgy energy that during this long hot summer had demanded some nameless release. The uncarpeted boards were cool and slippery beneath her bare feet as she ran to the open window where the morning air blew fresh and sweet. Slowly, she pushed her hands through the tumbled mane of her long dark hair, holding it up and away from her neck and shoulders. Today was special, very special.

She released the heavy mass of her hair and it settled back, cloaking her shoulders, almost reaching her waist; her eyes sparkled with secret anticipation.

Micah didn't hold with birthdays, or with Christmas, come to that, but Jet always managed to contrive some kind of celebration for herself. And today marked the turning point. From today she was no longer under Micah's legal guardianship. She could go, walk out of this comfortless, loveless house and never come back. She would make a life of her own, far away from the uncle who had begun by terrifying her and had ended up, twelve years on, by disgusting her.

Quite how she would accomplish her objective she didn't yet know. She hadn't a penny to her name, the few clothes she possessed were a local disgrace, and she'd had a very patchy education. But, on the other hand, she was fit and healthy and intelligent—so she'd find a way.

If Micah had kept money in the house she would have taken it. He owed her. For years now she'd worked like a slave around the farm, and never a penny paid in wages, never so much as a word of thanks or praise.

Working for nothing except blows and bad words was a thing of the past, and she'd spend today in the hills, as she'd promised herself, just as a birthday treat. And to make it easier, today was market day in Tolcaster. Micah never missed it. At that thought her vivid eyes flew open.

He would be up early, too, and he always took Prince to market with him.

Flying silently down the twisting stairs, her bare feet collecting dirt, she swooped into the kitchen and took the bowl of scraps from its hiding place under the sink. Quietly, so as not to alert Micah, she slipped the bolt on the back door and stepped out into the pink-tinged dawn.

The sheepdog came out of his rough kennel, shaking his dull coat, rattling his heavy chain, his eyes devoted. Stooping down, regardless of how the hem of her nightgown dragged in the dust of the unkempt yard, Jet gave him the scraps she'd saved for him, fondling the animal's ears as he ate, murmuring endearments.

Prince had been a puppy when Jet—six years old, frightened and grieving—had come here to live. Since there'd been no one else around who'd wanted the love Jet had cooped up inside her, she had given it all to the dog. And he had returned it a hundredfold. He was getting old now, stiff and rheumaticky, going blind. But he still worked the sheep and Micah would accord him no rest until the matter was taken out of his hands and the dog dropped dead.

Prince, his meal finished, rested his chin on her knees, his tail waving softly, his eyes melting with adoration. Jet's own eyes sparkled with sudden tears. What would happen to him when she left? He'd die, she just knew he would! There would be no one to supplement the sparse rations Micah doled out—when he remembered. No one to stuff his kennel with warm sweet hay when the wind blew cold over the hills. No one to give him a single affectionate word. She couldn't leave him behind, she simply couldn't bear the thought of his misery if she did, so she would have to take him with her. They'd manage, somehow.

Giving the old dog a final pat, Jet padded back inside.

Micah was already down and in the kitchen when she went through with the empty bowl. Holding the telltale evidence behind her—Micah would throw a fit if he ever discovered she fed 'decent human food' to that 'damned old dog'—she edged over to the table, depositing it gently amongst the rest of the clutter where she hoped it would remain unnoticed.

Micah looked up from the bacon he was frying for himself just as her fingers released the bowl, his small eyes narrowing. 'Why aren't you dressed? Trust you to flaunt yourself.'

Gulping, Jet crossed her arms over her breasts, the rosy points of the gently rounded globes discernible through the shoddy fabric of her darned old nightgown.

He was hateful! Disgusting! She wasn't flaunting herself, she just hadn't expected him to be up and about quite so early, that's all! And what was there to flaunt, anyway!

Tall, leggy, Jet had always been thin. This summer she'd started at last to grow a figure—as she described the softly swelling breasts and the more rounded outline of her boyish hips. And nameless longings sometimes filled her, making her edgy and desperate to break away from the slow strangulation of her loveless, aimless life.

Tossing her head, she stalked out of the kitchen, trying to look dignified, but as soon as she'd closed the door behind her she raced up the stairs and locked herself in her bedroom. She sat on the bed, her knees drawn up to her chin, until she heard the truck drive away. He was gone. It was her birthday. And she wasn't going to do a single one of the dozens of chores he'd listed for her last night!

As the sound of the engine faded she rolled over on her stomach and fished about under the bed until her fingers found the plastic carrier. Lovingly, she extracted the dress. She'd be blowed if she'd spend today—the most important one of her life to date—dressed in her normal drab get-up of old trousers and shirt!

As she held the vivid scarlet and yellow fabric against her cheek she recalled how pleased she'd been when she'd found it. She always helped out at the village jumble sales, she made sure she did, even though she knew the majority of the other helpers looked at her with disapproval, because right at the end the vicar's wife—who wasn't a bad old dear—allowed her to pick out one or two garments for her own use, free of charge. And at the last sale she'd chosen this dress, instead of the usual sensible working gear.

Moving quickly now Micah was out of the way, she dragged her nightgown over her head and slipped into the dress. It felt strange. She was eighteen and couldn't remember ever wearing a dress. At six years old she must have arrived with some, of course, and worn them until they'd dropped off her back, but she couldn't remember how it felt.

She gave an experimental twirl; the soft Indian cotton felt tickly against her bare legs, airy and light. Frowning a little, she tugged at the neckline. The elastic had gone, which was probably why it had ended up in the jumble, and the semi-transparent fabric flopped all over the place. If she pulled the bodice up so that the front was decent, then her shoulders protruded. And half her back. Talk about flaunting herself!

She gave a final twitch and left the room on winged bare feet. There would be no one up in the sun-soaked hills to notice whether the front of her dress gaped or not! And at least, on her eighteenth birthday, she felt like a woman instead of a farmhand of indeterminate sex.

She spent the morning wandering idly in the hills

which circled the old farmhouse, enjoying the sense of freedom, the crisp feel of the sun-dried grass beneath her feet, the unfamiliar gauzy softness of the dress as it moved with her, caressing the naked body beneath. When she was hungry she sat on an outcrop of rock and ate the thick cheese sandwiches she'd brought with her. She would miss the hills when she left; they had been her playground, her solace, for as long as she could clearly remember. But she couldn't stay on with Micah. There would be other hills to roam, other air to breathe.

Drowsily, she spread the cheap fabric of her gaudy dress around her and lay down, slipping into sleep as the sun grew high and brassy, waking to shiver as the first low mutter of thunder prowled the hills and the first large drops of rain hit her.

Jerking herself up on one elbow, pushing her tangled hair back from her face, she raised troubled eyes to the sky. It was an ominous heavy grey, and as if that wasn't enough, thunder rattled through the hills again, sounding closer.

Jet had taught herself not to be afraid of anything, but the fear of thunderstorms would never leave her. At six years old she'd been wide awake, scared, keeping the baby-sitter company because she'd seemed even more frightened than Jet, while a storm had raged around the house where she'd lived with her parents.

The police had come just as the storm had peaked. Both her parents had been killed when the oak tree at the end of the road, split by lightning, had fallen on their car as they'd been on their way home after a rare evening out. And ever since then no amount of reasoning with herself could keep the terror away when thunder roared and lightning spat.

She scrambled to her feet, ripping her dress, her heart thudding unbearably as a flash of lightning broke the sky. Her pupils dilated with instinctive terror, she slithered round the shoulder of the hill, making for the shepherd's hut and shelter.

It was a fair distance, but nearer than the farmhouse, and by the time she pushed open the flimsy wooden door her dress was in tatters, clinging to her, soaked by the downpour. Each rasping breath hurt now and, driven half out of her senses by her deep-seated fear, she hurled herself across the hay bales left over from last season's lambing, her wet hair splayed out like a pool of black water.

'Hey—that was quite an entrance!'

Jet heard the voice dimly, all mixed up with the menacing rumble of thunder, the rattle of the rain on the tin roof. She heard feet rustling in the hay and knew the man was standing over her as she burrowed into the scratchy bales like a half-crazed animal, intent only on hiding herself from the fury of the storm.

'Come on, now. Who's after you? Beelzebub?'

His hands were warm on her shoulders, pulling her out of her hiding place, firm but gentle. He was on his haunches and as he dragged her to a sitting position, pulling her bunched fists way from her eyes, she could see that his eyes were kind, golden and warm, his strong, tanned features softened by a quizzical half smile.

'You're afraid of the storm? Or has something else got you in this state?'

Her eyes were wide, glazed, her body tense. Lightning stabbed, momentarily filling the inside of the dark little hut with searing brilliance, and she threw herself forward, sobbing and clutching, burrowing her head into the warmth of his body.

'Hush now, baby, hush now.' His voice had a strangely warm hypnotic quality as he sat in the hay, cradling her in his arms, holding her gently, talking softly until gradually her sobs subdued into sniffs and hiccups. 'I'm here. I had to make a run for it, too. We'll keep each other company until it blows over. Don't be afraid. Please try not to be so afraid.'

His deep voice was soothing, as if he cared, his body warm and reassuring, his arms comforting. Jet hadn't been held and comforted since she was six years old and she abandoned herself without thought to the pleasure, the forgotten feeling of being cared for. She didn't know who the man was, but there could be no harm in a person as kind as this.

'You know,' he said quickly, his arms tightening around her as another flash penetrated the gloom of the hut, 'I think I've seen you before, walking in the hills. Do you live around here?'

Jet nodded mutely, her lips clamped together as she waited for the inevitable crack of thunder. But her fingers were splayed out against his chest now, not claw-like and frenziedly clutching, and she could hear the steady beat of his heart, smell the musky male scent of him, feel his warmth beneath her cheek, against her body as he held her.

She shivered and snuggled closer. In some inexplicable way she was no longer so frightened of the storm. It was as if, by holding her, giving back the comforting reassurance that had been so tragically taken from her by that other, long-ago storm, he had removed the fear.

'Lucky you,' he said as he felt her nod. 'It's a beautiful part of the country. I stay here with friends whenever I can scrape some time together—at Withington Manor— do you know it?' His hands stroked her shoulders, gentling her, as thunder rolled again through the hills. 'It isn't far from here.'

As the crow flew, the village of Withington was three miles over the hills. Withington Manor was a little closer.

Looking down from the hillside, you could see it, a jewel in masoned stone, set in immaculate parkland.

'I've seen it,' Jet murmured against his shirt, the first words she'd spoken to him coming stiffly. She had seen the house, but only from the outside. The likes of her didn't get invited to places like that. 'Hilda Briggs is the housekeeper there; her sister runs our village post office,' she told him.

'That almost counts as a formal introduction,' he replied, sounding amused. 'I'm Denzil Fox, by the way— but you can call me Denny. Won't you tell me your name?'

'Jet. Jet Luellyn.'

'Jet. For your hair?' His strong, lean fingers touched her wet locks, straying through them idly, finding her warm nape. His other hand was still on her back, holding her, but its gentling movements were suddenly erotic.

She made a small whimpering sound of pleasure, enjoying the new and delightful sensations his caressing fingers created in her. Her eyes closing, she moved closer, innocently snuggling against him, her body wriggling with unknowing provocation.

But even as her hands clung to him, drawing the comfort of his presence closer, he got to his feet in one swift movement, walking away from her across the hay-littered floor space, and she held out her arms, crying instinctively, 'Don't leave me! Don't go!'

She was shaking again, and it wasn't because she was afraid of the storm—she was afraid of losing whatever it was he'd been offering, afraid and she didn't know why.

'I'm not going anywhere.' His voice was older, harder, and it made her want to cry. 'You're soaking wet, child,' he said at last.

'I'm not a child!' She sounded ten years old. 'I'm eighteen today.'

'So ancient!' The smile was back in his voice; that made her feel happier, and she scrambled eagerly to her feet when he held out a hand to help her up. 'Take that wet thing off—your dress, or whatever.'

Looking down at herself, she could understand why he had difficulty knowing what to call the soggy, clinging garment. Even in the ghostly half-light she could see that the gaudy colours had run, that it was more torn than whole, the front of the bodice, predictably, sagging. Jet tugged frantically at the wet material, covering herself, trying to joke.

'You shouldn't call it a "whatever"! It's my best dress—my only dress, as a matter of fact! And if it looks like a rag, well, okay, I'm used to wearing rags!' She'd meant to make him laugh, but he wasn't even smiling. The look he was giving her from his beautiful golden eyes was long and considering, and she babbled, suddenly confused, 'And I can't take it off because there's nothing underneath.'

Her teeth were chattering and she was shaking again because he'd withdrawn the warmth of his comfort, mentally as well as physically. She thought he swore, but wasn't sure, but she heard the tight-lipped command, 'Wear my shirt. I got here before the rain really started so it's dry. If you stay in that wet thing you'll get pneumonia.'

He turned his back on her, already unbuttoning his shirt, tugging it out of the waistband of his jeans.

There seemed nothing else for it but to do as he said. She couldn't bear him to be angry with her, and she couldn't understand why he was. Shakily, she pulled the dress over her head, hearing the wet fabric split again. It dropped to the floor and she stood naked, shivering convulsively, staring at the hard, tapering line of his back, the wide shoulders down to the narrow trim waist, the tanned skin gleaming in the dim light.

He held out the shirt in the fingers of one hand, his back still to her, sounding irritable as he shook the garment. 'Put it on. I won't turn round until you say so.'

Jet made a grab for the shirt, wriggling into it, her fingers fumbling with the buttons, her eyes on his back. Buttons didn't seem to fit into buttonholes; her hands were shaking too much. Giving up the attempt, she hugged the fabric to her, inhaling the clean male scent it carried, guessing at his impatience from the way his shoulder muscles clenched.

'I'm decent now,' she told him timidly, hoping he wasn't still cross with her, and he turned slowly, reluctantly, at her words, his eyes travelling from the jet hair, that emphasised the delicate loveliness of her features, to the long bare legs exposed by the shirt.

'Fine.' His expression unreadable, he turned again, going to the one small window, staring out through the layer of grime and cobwebs which had hay seeds clinging to them. 'The storm's passing. It shouldn't be too long before this damn rain stops and we can go.'

He sounded as if he couldn't wait to leave. Jet felt bereft; the comfort he'd offered, the warmth of his caring had been too abruptly withdrawn from the girl who had known nothing of either for the last twelve years.

She made a sound of polite assent but it came out as a whimper as a sudden crack of thunder reverberated in the hills.

Denny turned then, quickly, his face concerned, and the rain clattered on the roof, filling the hut with the remorseless rhythm of its sound. Even so, she heard his sigh, saw the slight relaxation of his taut body as he held out his arms to her. Choking inside with some inexplicable emotion, Jet fled over the scattered hay, wanting his comfort, sighing blissfully as his arms came around her and he sank to the floor, pulling her with him. Her arms were clinging as she pressed closer, her hands going up to tangle in his crisp fox-shadow hair, the thick feel of it between her fingers making her heart thud faster.

'Do you know what you're doing, Jet?' His voice was unsteady, thick, and she lifted her face to the curve of his neck, her lips moving against his throat where she could feel the heavy beating of a pulse.

She had no answer to make to his question. She didn't really know what he meant by it. She only knew that what was happening felt right, so right, as if she'd been waiting for him to hold her for a long, long time.

Denny's hand moved softly on her naked hip, his mouth finding hers, making her go weak with pleasure at the sensual movement as he parted her lips. She responded with eager innocence, craving the warmth and affection she'd been denied for so long, following the insistent dictates of her burgeoning sensuality, conscious only of the wild intensity of her need.

'Denny . . . Oh, Denny . . .!' His name was dragged from her in a throaty whisper as he removed the shirt, pushing her gently back against the hay. His hands were strong, but they were shaking, his face harder, his expression intent as his eyes devoured the pale loveliness of her body.

Jet had never felt like this before, drowning in pulsating sensation. She could hear his ragged breathing mingled with the drumming of the rain on the roof, hear the frantic pounding of her own heart beats. There was tension inside the hut, the warm damp air was full of it and she broke it instinctively as she held out her arms to him, her eyes burning in her flushed face, the unknown need overpowering her, bursting into an untamed explosion of wanting as he covered her, skin searing skin, lips searching and fusing.

It was quite dark in the little hut when Denny said
thickly, 'It was your first time, wasn't it, Jet?'

She thought he sounded unsteady, as if what had
happened had shaken him. Cradled in the curve of his
arm, her legs imprisoned beneath his, Jet felt too relaxed
to move. She wanted to stay where she was for ever. She
loved him and she had been waiting for him all her life.
Her head was against his chest, her lips parted, tasting
his skin. She could hear his heartbeats, feel the
dependability of solid muscle and bone beneath her
splayed fingers. And she loved him. Oh, how she loved
him!

Sometimes, dreaming her solitary dreams in the hills,
she had imagined a handsome stranger, a mystical being
who would make her his own, care for her, love her. And
now the dream had come true.

'Mmmmm,' she answered his question drowsily. 'I
suppose so.'

'There can't be any "suppose" about it.' She didn't like
the new edginess in his voice. It worried her. Everything,
just for this one night, had to be perfect. Mystical beings
could vanish as quickly as they had appeared, but until
he did go, everything had to be perfect. Smothering the
soft giggle produced by the zany path her thoughts were
taking her, she nuzzled his chest, putting soft kisses on
his warm, moist skin, feeling him tremble.

'Well, I have been kissed.' Jet didn't want him to know
how green she was, knowing instinctively that it would
trouble him. And Alan had kissed her. Once. A hurried,
clumsy kiss, planted on her mouth just before his parents
had arrived to take him home at the end of his holiday
from agricultural college, two weeks ago. The only
sensation she had experienced then had been surprise.

'A regular boyfriend?'

She felt his body tense and shook her head. 'Not particularly. There's no one special.' She didn't want to talk about Alan. What had happened between her and Denny had been too wonderful, too precious to spoil with talk of anyone else, and her eyes filled up with tears as he carefully removed her clinging hands and sat up, his head in his hands, his back turned to her.

'It's been a first time for me, too.' His voice was muffled, filled with self-loathing. 'I don't mean it's the first time I've made love to a woman—after all, I'm twenty-eight years old! But I've never taken a virgin. I've never made love to any woman a few minutes after meeting her!'

The tears spilled over then, burning her eyes. He was sorry it had happened, disgusted with himself. Perhaps he was disgusted with her, too. She couldn't bear that! To him their loving was something to be ashamed of, while to her it was the most beautiful thing that had ever happened.

He must have caught the sound of the sob she'd tried to swallow because he turned swiftly, gathering her into his arms. 'Don't cry. Don't cry, sweetheart.' He said it over and over, kissing away the falling tears, groaning, 'How can anything that seemed so right be so wrong!'

For a time they held each other, clinging to the only reality there was. The storm had finally passed and the evening air blowing in through a broken pane in the tiny window was sweet and pure. After a while they talked, although Jet didn't give him more than the bare outlines of her life, because up until now her existence had no meaning for her. But she hung on every detail he told her, storing every word away in her mind for later, more leisurely savouring.

He was unattached, with a father and sister living in

Bournemouth. He was a journalist with one of the more prestigious national dailies and he came as often as possible to Withington to stay with friends. He liked classical guitar music, fast cars, pizzas, most modern poets and hang-gliding.

'And you, of course. I rather care for you!' He ran a finger along her perfectly moulded profile, pausing, tantalisingly, on her parted lips.

'Do you? Do you really like me?' Jet whispered, her mouth trembling as he traced the outline of her full lower lip.

'Yes, really. And do you like me, just a little, in spite of what I did to you?'

'I love you!' She deplored the doubt in his voice and exploded with a savagery she hadn't known she could feel in connection with him. 'It did take two of us! And it was beautiful. So don't talk as if it was something shameful! I love you ... I love you, Denny ...'

The second time he made love to her it was with a tenderness that made her cry for the beauty of it, for the strange magic of love.

He kissed her tears away as if he understood the reason for them, his voice deep with emotion as he told her, 'I didn't know love could happen so quickly, so perfectly. I didn't know it could be like this—I feel as if I never knew anything worth knowing before, it's like being reborn. It's real, Jet, and it's for ever.'

Jet stirred, a deep shudder running through her. The sky had clouded over, and the long hot afternoon had vanished in the chilling aftermath of memory. She was stiff from sitting for so long in one position and she unwound her long legs carefully, wincing with the pain of cramped muscles, her heart contracting with the greater pain of remembering just how it had been for Denny and her.

They had left the hut as the pale fingers of dawn slid across the sky. They had been so happy, as natural with each other as healthy young animals—and nothing of what had happened seemed sordid or wrong, not then, simply a mystical, beautiful, loving thing that had let the spirit soar free.

Denny had been full of plans, and she had listened, practically inarticulate with wondering joy. He still had ten days of his holiday left, and they'd spend the time getting to know each other. Jet felt that she knew all there was to know about him; he was the other half of herself.

When his holiday was over he'd take her back to London with him and they'd marry there. He had a flat—smallish, but big enough for two. Two and a dog, he promised her then, laughing at her delight because she had told him about poor old Prince and he had remembered and cared.

'And while I'm out earning crusts you'll think of me and walk the dog, and think of me.'

It sounded like heaven to Jet, all the lost high spots of her life, the happiness and love that should have been hers but hadn't, rolled into one unbelievably wonderful package.

Denny insisted on telling Micah of their plans, though Jet hadn't been sure about that. He would only try to spoil her happiness. Not that he could, of course, but he didn't think happiness was part of the human condition and she didn't want to hear his foul tongue clacking about the man she loved. Micah, much as he disliked her, wouldn't want to lose an unpaid worker, the butt for his ill-humour, and would do everything he could to taint her joy.

'I'll have some explaining to do back at Withington,' Denny told her as the rooftop of Foundlands came in sight over the brow of the hill. 'I'll tell them I spent the night with my future wife—you won't mind?'

She shook her head, her eyes dark with love, and he grinned suddenly, holding her at arm's length. 'What sights we look!'

'You look fine.' Her eyes devoured his tall, lithe, perfectly proportioned body dressed in just his denim jeans and sneakers, wanting to touch, seeing the quick flare of his own need in the golden eyes.

Looking away, suddenly circumspect because any minute now Micah might come out looking for her, cursing because her bed hadn't been slept in and the day's chores hadn't been started on.

'I'm the sight, not you. And if you don't care, I don't.'

She was barefoot, wearing his shirt, which was crumpled now and stained with the dye that had run from her dress. She'd tied that gaudy garment round her waist, making a bizarre skirt of it, and she told him, 'All my clothes are tatty. Second-hand trousers and tops. I only ever had one skirt. That was when I started at the secondary school; it was part of the uniform so Micah had to fork out then. He gave Mrs Briggs the money— you know, she's your friends' housekeeper now, only she was helping her sister in our village post office in those days; it was before her husband died. Anyway, Micah asked her to take me to town and buy what was essential. I never had another skirt. When I grew too big for that one he made me sew bits on. It ended up like a patchwork quilt—only not so nice. I'm only telling you this,' she said, very serious now, 'so you'll know what to expect. I don't want you to be ashamed of me.'

'I couldn't be ashamed of you!' The words were quick and angry, Denny's face set in hard lines that frightened her. 'You shall have all the clothes you want. Beautiful clothes.'

'I only want you,' Jet whispered uncertainly, distressed by the anger she sensed in him, unable to understand it.

'Oh Jet . . .' His eyes softened, darkening. 'You just don't know the way I feel, do you?' He pulled her roughly into his arms, holding her against his lean hard length, his voice heavy with desire, 'Tell me you love me. Say, "I love you, Denny"—say it, Jet!'

Jet negotiated the steep sheep track, down through the whin, her face set, her body tormented by the pain she'd imagined over and done with long ago. That other self, the long-gone blithe child who'd been Jet Luellyn, had been so happy that day. She'd sung as she worked around the farm, unable to stop smiling even when Micah was grumbling at her—which he mostly was when he was around. Denny had said he would call that afternoon to tell Micah that they were to be married. He would come at four.

But he hadn't. Of course he hadn't. Jet's mouth was grim, her eyes hard. He had taken what he'd wanted, had his night of pleasure, and disappeared. She recalled how she'd waited, waited and hoped, right up until gone midnight. The following days had crawled by and still she'd waited, unable to eat or sleep or to stay still for longer than a few seconds. She had haunted the hillside, watching, hoping, edgy—afraid that something dreadful had happened to him, afraid of the other thing, the thing she couldn't bring herself to face.

When a week had passed she had gone to Withington. If he wouldn't or couldn't come to her, then she would go to him. His holiday would soon be over. She had gone across the hills, hovering near the Manor's impressive iron gates, too miserable to approach, so nervous that she felt sick. At last she'd plucked up the courage the only way she knew how—by mentally reliving that night when she'd found the only man she would ever love, by telling herself that he loved her, too.

Mrs Briggs had opened the door to her knock, her face looking anxious when she recognised the girl, and Jet said, mumbling her words, 'Is—is Denny Fox here, please? Could I see him, just for a minute?'

'Jet dear, don't you think——'

But a sharp sophisticated voice, just in the background, had broken through the housekeeper's words and Jet, twisting her hands nervously together, watched Mrs Briggs walk away, her relief evident.

'Well, what is it?'

Jet had raised her eyes to see the most beautiful woman she had ever clapped eyes on. Pamela Trent, daughter of the house, was well known in the vicinity for her looks. 'Knock spots off any film star' was the local consensus. Jet had never seen her at close quarters, and her eyes widened in admiration for the sheer loveliness of coiled golden hair, the perfect figure clad in something long and silky, the colour of purple grapes.

'What is it?' The question was repeated impatiently. 'Aren't you the Luellyn brat from Tipper's Batch way?'

Jet nodded, catching in a deep breath and a hint of expensive perfume. 'I've come to see Mr Fox. Denny Fox, please.'

'Oh?' Pamela Trent's smile hadn't been pleasant. 'I'm sorry, my fiancé, Denny, isn't in at the moment. But I'll make sure he gets your message, if you'd like to leave it with me.'

Jet had never been able to remember the walk back to Foundlands. Her brief spell of happiness in her love for him had had the quality of every great and soaring joy, but the pain, the sense of deep betrayal, transcended even that.

The love she had given him had been pure and innocent. If he had said goodbye in the dawn she could have accepted that. It would have hurt but she would have understood and would have kept the purity of her love for him locked secretly away in her heart for the rest of her life, thankful that she had at least once known love.

But he had said he loved her too, wanted to marry her, live with her always. And that was unforgivable. How he must have laughed at her stupidity! She felt cheap, unclean, and what had been the most wonderful experience of her short life now seemed shoddy and sordid.

# CHAPTER FIVE

As she walked in the front door she heard Barbie's voice coming from the kitchen, then Alan laughing at something she'd said. Jet hadn't been expecting him but he came over as often as he could on an open-ended invitation. She didn't bother to go through to tell them she was home but went up the stairs slowly, like an old woman, meeting Ben stumping down them in his pyjamas, ready for bed.

'Hi, Ben,' she greeted him automatically, seeing from the corner of her eye the way the child politely flattened himself against the wall, giving her room to pass on the narrow staircase, his normally expressive face blank.

Jet was the only person with whom Ben was unnaturally quiet, instinctively well-behaved. She knew her aloofness repressed him but couldn't bring herself to try for any kind of rapport. It wasn't that she disliked children; in fact, Ben's existence had been the deciding factor when she'd chosen Barbie out of half a dozen others equally suitable for the job as live-in secretary and general help. She knew from experience that single parent families often had a rough ride through life.

But she couldn't get close to the child; she dared not. To have done so would have brought home Tod's loss to her with a poignancy she knew she couldn't bear.

When the bathroom door was closed behind her she slowly removed her ruined clothes, moving like an automaton, and stepped under the shower. The stinging needles of hot water scarcely registered. The catharsis of remembering had left her empty, not feeling anything

68

except drained and utterly weary. Sooner or later the pain would come back because it wouldn't be so easy to block out the memories a second time around. In the meantime there was the evening to get through—supper with Alan and Barbie.

'Remind me to go shopping for slacks and walking shoes.' Jet helped herself to salad from the glass bowl and winced at the size of the slice of quiche Barbie had put on her plate. 'I ruined a perfectly good skirt out walking this afternoon.'

She was doing her best to appear normal, because she had seen Alan and Barbie exchange odd looks when, ten minutes after joining them in the sitting-room before supper, she had realised she was acting like a zombie. She still felt like one, but was trying to hide it, prattling of this and that, only taking any real interest in the conversation when Barbie said, 'Alan's asked me out for a drink, Jet. Would you mind baby-sitting?'

'I thought it would be a good way for her to get to know a few of the locals,' Alan put in quickly, his light eyes almost apologetic. 'I'd have asked you both, but——' His words tailed off and Jet smiled.

'Go ahead. Ben's no trouble and I really ought to get down to some work.'

She had noticed the way Alan looked at Barbie from time to time: male speculation turning to something warmer and deeper as his visits to Foundlands had grown in number. He was an attractive man with a personality to match: warm and caring. If Alan could take her mind off her meeting with her 'Heavenly Man', the despicable Denny Fox, then Jet would do all she could in the way of encouragement.

'And don't hurry back,' she added, stacking dishes.

'I'll see to the washing up—you two go out and have a good time.'

'Ben's already asleep,' said Barbie. 'I looked in on him earlier and he was out for the count. If you're sure you don't mind?'

'Just go!' Jet forced a grin. Feeling was coming back and she had to do something to block it. She practically threw the other two out of the house, then cleared up and washed up at full stretch, almost running to the study where she put all that tight-wire energy into concentrating on the beginning pages of the new book.

But later, in bed, there was no way she could keep Denny out of her head. The pain of the old heartbreak came back, as if his betrayal had happened yesterday, and she cried herself to sleep, which was something she hadn't done in years.

Waking cold-eyed and calm, Jet reminded herself that what had happened between herself and Denny was old history. She had successfully put it out of her mind once, and could do the same again. No hassle. All it took was willpower and the sense to recognise him for the rat he was. Why he should so obviously hate her, call her a 'half-tamed scrubber' and a 'two-timing whore', was beyond her, and didn't concern her because to her he was less than nothing. And when she saw him again—which she supposed was inevitable—she would let him see that he was less than nothing.

There wasn't much post, just a cheque and a covering letter from her agent and a query from her UK publisher regarding the new book's progress. She handed them over to Barbie to deal with, and as Barbie and Ben sat down to cereal and toast Jet carried her coffee through to the study, pausing at the door, remembering to ask, 'Did you have a good time last night?'

'Yes, great! The village pub's like something out of Dickens! We had a lovely evening. Tell you all about it later.'

Jet left the room, smiling. Alan must have made a real impression. The village pub was quaint but it didn't merit all those stars in Barbie's eyes!

She worked solidly until noon, her powers of concentration coming back. She surfaced with difficulty when Barbie brought through the bowl of clear soup which was all the lunch Jet ever bothered with when deep in the creative effort of the all-important first draft.

'Going okay?' It was what Barbie usually said when the work was in its first stages, and she usually went away after that because she knew Jet's mind was on another plane. But today she hovered, moving restlessly from one foot to the other, her eyes bright.

Jet, recognising the signs, said resignedly, 'Out with it! I can tell there's something you're bursting to say.'

'Well——' Barbie drew the word out, perching on the desk, twisting a glossy curl round one finger then releasing it again like a spring.

All settled in for the duration, Jet supposed, smiling to herself, guessing she was in for a blow-by-blow account of last night's happenings. She sipped soup absently, her eyes affectionate as Barbie gabbled, 'Now promise you won't get stroppy, Jet, but Alan and I talked it over last night and decided it was time you had a bit of relaxation. So we're going to treat you to an evening out, and we've booked a table at that new restaurant between the village and Tolcaster, The Plume Of Feathers, for tomorrow night. They do a fabulous menu and there's dancing.'

She paused for breath, her brown eyes slightly apprehensive, and Jet commented drily, 'Is there now!' She finished her soup and put the empty bowl on her desk. 'And what happens about Ben?' Or is he included in this therapeutic expedition?'

'Don't be so daft!' Barbie pulled a long-suffering face.
'It's all taken care of. I'm to take him over to Alan's place
some time tomorrow afternoon, and he can stay
overnight and through till Sunday evening. Alan said his
mum would love to have him. And Ben will be over the
moon when I tell him—you know how much he enjoyed
himself when he went over last Sunday—and Mrs Taylor
made such a fuss of him.'

'So the matter's out of my hands.' Jet shrugged,
smiling, though, thinking that maybe they were right at
that. It was a long time since she'd been out for an
evening, and it should be fun.

'Then it's all fixed?' Barbie's head was tilted on one
side, her eyes narrowed. 'No fuss? No elaborate
excuses?'

'No, no fuss. It was sweet of you both to think of it; I'd
love to go. However——' she slanted a brilliant blue
amused look, 'are you sure you won't mind a third party
along, playing gooseberry?'

'That's all taken care of, too!' Barbie slipped down
from the desk top, her gurgle of laughter childlike and
unaffected. 'Denny Fox is making up the four. We're
meeting him there at eight.' And because she took Jet's
silence, the quality of watchful stillness that surrounded
her, as an indication of wanting to know more, she
prattled on. 'After we'd had a couple of drinks at the local
Alan suggested we went on to The Plume Of Feathers.
It's only recently been opened and he wanted to see what
it was like. It was super, so we got the idea of taking you
there, and Denny happened to be at the bar. He joined us
and Alan told him we were thinking of bringing you
there on Saturday night, and I don't know who actually
suggested it but Denny's coming too. What's wrong?'
Barbie's forehead puckered as she peered into Jet's still

face, the mouth pulled to a thin hard line. 'Why the frosty look? You two do know each other, after all. He said you'd met before that day he came here for coffee.' Her eyes twinkled wickedly. 'He's so gorgeous—I thought you might like the idea of getting re-acquainted!'

Getting re-acquainted! Jet's mouth went dry, her heart thumping sickeningly. If only Barbie knew what she was saying! And there was no way she could back out now, not after saying she'd love to go, not without making explanations she had no intention of giving. She picked up Barbie's first point, the words coming out with difficulty.

'We met, briefly, when Mr Fox came here to ask Alan if he could buy this place privately. But I'd already decided to buy it, so the meeting was terse, to say the least.' It was a garbled version of the truth and left a great deal out, but it would stop Barbie from asking where and when they'd met before.

'Ummmm.' The other girl gave Jet a long considering look. 'So that makes him still a stranger in your book. And you don't relax with strangers—especially if they're the male variety; I know that much about you. I also know that men are like so much wallpaper as far as you're concerned. I used to be like that, too. For the past five years men have been little more than shadows in suits, or whatever. But I've at last woken up to the fact that the entire male population didn't die when Toby did. So come on.' Her eyes snapped out of the musing state. 'I don't know why you don't take any interest in men— that's your business—but I think it's high time you started. Some of them are quite nice! Denny Fox, for example. You've got to agree that he's potent stuff, and he's kind, too, which makes it better. And he knows how to put people at their ease, so you won't end the evening feeling he's still a stranger.'

Barbie sat down again, extolling Denny's finer points as she saw them, and Jet thought, Go away! I don't want to hear! But she kept quiet, grimly listening, knowing that all the starry-eyed euphoria hadn't been for Alan, for the good time they'd had last night, the prospect of spending tomorrow evening in his company. It was all down to Denny, and the thought of it made Jet want to throw up.

'Apparently he used to be a journalist,' Barbie was saying. 'But now he produces his own TV documentary series and runs a private world-wide news syndicate. He's come a long way in a short time—he's thirty-four, by the way, not married, and——'

So what happened to the gorgeous Pamela Trent, Jet wondered acidly, shutting out the flow of Barbie's chatter. Six years ago they'd been engaged to be married. Had he been forced to buy her an engagement ring before being allowed to possess that beautiful body? That must have really irked him when there were half-tamed scrubbers like Jet Luellyn around, only too ready and eager to fall into his arms, brainless enough to listen to his promises of undying love, gullible enough to believe them!

Jet's mouth twisted bitterly, her eyes narrowed to slits of inky ice. She pulled a sheaf of papers towards her and reached for a pen. Taking her dismissal easily, but getting the reason for it wrong, Barbie scrambled to her feet.

'Sorry; I'll let you get on. I didn't intend to break the flow, but I did want to tell you about tomorrow evening. Oh, by the way,' she paused at the door, smiling over her shoulder, 'if you don't need me this afternoon, could I slip into Tolcaster? I'll need something special to wear for tomorrow.'

Jet gritted her teeth; the little fool was heading for

disaster if she thought she could get Denny Fox seriously interested in her. He'd be interested, that went without saying, but it wouldn't ever get serious. She re-shuffled the papers, looking engrossed. 'Take all the time you need.'

The face reflected back from the full-length mirror on the bathroom wall was white with strain, the fine skin drawn tight across the high cheekbones, the eyes huge and dark, over-bright with tension.

Jet turned from the mirror with a disgusted snort and sat down heavily on the rim of the bath, her towel wrapped round her like a sarong. Why did she let him get to her this way? He was a rat and a louse and he didn't merit this emotional upheaval. Barbie had said she couldn't recall whose suggestion it had been that Denny should join their party. Jet knew. He was muscling in on her life for his own devilish reasons, using Barbie. Though what he hoped to gain from this cat-and-mouse game, she didn't know. Who knew what went on in his twisted, cheating mind?

Up until an hour ago when Barbie had driven an excited Ben over to Alan's farm where he was to stay overnight and through Sunday, Jet had been determined to skip the evening at The Plume Of Feathers. Why should she be forced into spending time in Denny's company when all she wanted to do was forget he existed?

She looked awful enough for a last-minute excuse of a sudden migraine attack to hold water. But before she'd left with Ben, Barbie hadn't been able to resist trying on her new dress for Jet's approval. She had pranced around the kitchen, the full skirts of the jade-green chiffon dress swirling around her calves, the bodice making her waist look nothing, leaving her shoulders bare. And there had been a glow of excitement in her brown eyes that had turned Jet's stomach over. She was embarking on a roller-coaster ride to heartbreak and there was nothing Jet could do about it.

What woman, in the first delirious stages of infatuation, would listen to a friend's advice, however well meant? Even if Jet confided the whole sordid story, Barbie wouldn't listen. Every woman likes to believe she can tame the particular monster she's chosen—even if dozens before her have failed.

Waving the pair of them off a short time later, Jet had known that she had to forget the idea of a manufactured migraine. If she couldn't warn Barbie away from Denny, she could tell him to stay away from her friend. She wasn't going to stand on the sidelines and watch Denny break Barbie up as he had once broken her.

She would threaten to tell Barbie and anyone else who would listen exactly what he'd done six years ago. And even if it didn't change Barbie's attitude towards him, his name would be mud in this area and the inhabitants of his adopted village would despise him, because attitudes in this isolated hill-farming area were still highly moralistic, rooted in the nineteenth century.

She took special care with her make-up because she looked like death, then zipped up the black jersey silk sleeveless dress, fastening a brooch that was the exact colour of her eyes to the deep cowled neckline then fixed matching droppers to her ears. Twisting her hair into a loose knot on top of her head, Edwardian fashion, she viewed the finished result in the mirror with satisfaction. She looked controlled, sophisticated, expensive—a world away from the cheap scrubber of Denny's warped mind, she assured herself with a savagery that came from deep within her. And her confidence was bolstered when Alan, behind the wheel of his modest saloon, remarked,

'You should have kept the BMW, Jet. The way you're looking you shouldn't be travelling in anything less.'

'And what form of transport do you reckon I rate?' asked Barbie from the passenger seat at his side, turning to wink at Jet who was sitting behind. 'A horse and cart?'

'Who's fishing?' Alan grinned, refusing to be drawn, but his smile was the contented one of a man who has found what he'd been looking for. And that smile did as much as anything else to stiffen Jet's determination to tell Denny Fox to get lost, because given a fair crack of the whip Alan could bring Barbie to the point of returning his feelings.

He was already in the elegantly furnished, discreetly lit bar when they arrived. Jet's heart flipped over, her eyes homing straight in on him. He had no right to look so startlingly attractive, his wide shoulders and lean hips emphasised by the superb cut of the dark suit he wore, the immaculate whiteness of his shirt making his tanned skin seem darker, his hair crisper, richer.

He turned when he heard Barbie's cheery, 'Hi there, Denny!' and they drifted to a quiet table in an alcove. When they were seated he attracted a waiter's attention, ordering drinks, asking to see the menu, and he said, 'You look ravishing, Barbie,' but his eyes didn't leave Jet's face.

She drank her dry Martini quickly. She needed to do something to blank off the awareness of him that threaded through her veins like barbed quicksilver, so she drank another because it seemed like a good idea.

He was behaving impeccably, his charm and urbanity right on the surface. There was nothing to hint at the raw hatred he felt for her. But she knew it was there; she'd seen it before, in his eyes, heard it in his voice, tasted it on his lips . . .

Jet shied away from that thought, her eyes bleak. A
tremor of nervous tension rippled over her skin, and
Denny touched the naked flesh of her arm, his fingers
feather-light and lingering. 'Cold, Jet?'

'No. No, I'm fine.' She flinched away from him and
felt hot colour crawl over her face, met Barbie's puzzled
eyes and determinedly launched herself into an act that
comprised light conversation with just the right amount
of amused detachment and slight soft smiles that gave
nothing away.

When Denny suggested they went in to eat she rose
gracefully to her feet, knowing she wouldn't be able to
swallow a thing because the knot inside her was
tightening all the time. Denny led the way through to the
restaurant, his hand on Barbie's elbow, her bright face
turned up to his, her head tipped to catch what he was
saying.

'I'm looking forward to this,' remarked Alan cheerfully at her side. 'I'm starving! Doesn't Barbie look pretty?
You wouldn't think she was old enough to have a five-
year-old son.'

'She looks lovely,' agreed Jet tersely. Didn't the silly
idiot know what was going on? Couldn't he sense the
build-up to the great seduction that was being enacted in
front of his nose? But he didn't know Denny as she did.
All Alan would see was a man being attentive to an
attractive woman. But hadn't he noticed how Denny's
eyes flirted with Barbie but turned to stone when he
looked at her?

'Barbie tells me you're a writer of some repute.'
Denny's eyes were sardonic as they held Jet's across the
table, his smile very slightly contemptuous, as if he didn't
believe she was capable of writing a shopping list.

Jet met Barbie's eyes, saw the small negative shake of
her head and knew the secret identity of Roger Blye

hadn't been divulged. She gave her attention to the slice of chilled melon she was pushing around her plate as Denny, his starter finished, leaned back in his seat and prodded, 'I can't say I've ever come across a book by Jet Luellyn. Perhaps I could borrow a copy?' His tone was smooth, but his eyes needled her. 'Or you could give me the name of your publisher and your latest title and I could buy one. You probably think I should pay for my pleasures?'

The double meaning behind his words sent colour running over her cheekbones. He had previously implied that she was some kind of high-class tart, and now the need to lash out at him was strong. She put her spoon down and slowly, deliberately lifted her wine glass, looking at him over the rim, her eyes expressionless.

'Yes, I think you should pay for your pleasures. But I very much doubt whether you ever do.'

'Who's for more wine? Barbie? Jet?' Alan topped up the glasses, his smile forced, his face pink. Then he and Barbie began talking at once, their words quick, both trying to ease the situation they didn't understand.

Jet contributed little to the conversation during the meal, and ate less. The superb food grew cold on her plate as she drank more wine than was sensible. But the unaccustomed intake of alcohol did little for her, didn't relax her in any way she'd hoped it might. She was still stingingly aware of Denny, of every slight movement he made, of every inflexion of his voice, of every breath he took. They might have been the only two people here, locked in an emotional capsule that no one else could enter—except for the fact that, for him, she was invisible.

After that double-edged remark he'd made earlier, he hadn't said a word to her, or looked in her direction. All his charm, attention and easy conversation was given to the other two. Jet wished she could dismiss him from her thoughts as easily, and deplored the weakness in her that made her as aware of him as if he were an extension of herself.

There were a few couples on the small dance floor now; the music was soft and slow. Denny stood up, holding out a hand to Barbie, his smile persuasive. 'Dance with me?'

Jet half turned, facing Alan, her back towards the dance area. She didn't want to see Barbie in Denny's arms. Alan said, 'Nice place, this. We needed something just a little bit special in this area. Enjoying yourself?'

Jet said, 'Yes thank you,' very politely, trying to smile. She sipped her coffee and wished she hadn't come. The evening, already interminable, was likely to go on for hours yet.

'You ought to relax more often,' Alan told her, concern written all over his open face. 'Barbie says you're stretched so tightly these days you're likely to snap.'

'She's talking through her hat.'

Jet's smile was brittle, the disclaimer automatic. And if Alan thought she was relaxing now he wasn't seeing straight. He was drinking brandy with his coffee, his skin slightly flushed, his voice gently scolding as he told her, 'I think Denny was miffed when you wouldn't tell him about your books. It was on the tip of my tongue to let him in on the secret.'

She replied repressively, 'I'm glad you didn't.'

'I know that. I think you're nuts. If I'd made my name doing something, anything, I'd want the world to know how clever I was.'

'You know how I feel about it. I like my privacy.' And I don't want Denny Fox invading it, she thought bitterly, any more than he is already. She shrugged. 'It takes all sorts, so let's forget it. By the way,' she changed the subject, 'how's that new land drainage scheme coming along?'

Alan would happily talk for hours about his farm. He had put some extensive modernisation plans in operation after his father's death, borrowing heavily to finance his ideas, and was still almost childishly pleased because everything was paying off. But eventually even his enthusiasm for the topic wore thin and his eyes strayed regularly to the space beyond Jet's shoulders, his eyes slightly hurt.

Jet had been keenly aware of the passage of time, the changing tempo of the music as one dance ended and another began. Denny, most certainly, wouldn't dream of allowing Alan a fair crack of the whip!

'He's giving Barbie a good time.' Alan's voice was heavy, his head sunk down on his shoulders. 'Would you like to dance? I should have asked before, but you know me—get me on the subject of the farm and I forget everything else.'

'No thanks,' Jet smiled, adding lightly, 'why don't you cut in? Dance with Barbie—it's a free country.'

'I'm not up up to that kind of competition. I've got two left feet.'

She smiled at his dour tone then turned reluctantly, seeing what he meant. Denny and Barbie were moving as one to the sensuous rhythm, their steps perfectly attuned, her bright head resting against the dark fabric that clothed his wide shoulders, her expression dreamy.

A stab of something fierce and hot thrust sharply through Jet's body, curling her insides in a tight knot of raw jealousy. Appalled by the manic nature of her reaction, she closed her eyes, shuddering. She couldn't be jealous! She couldn't! It was madness of the most self-destructive kind.

Releasing a long unsteady breath, she turned her back

on the dance floor and accepted a cigarette from the pack Alan was offering her. Inhaling deeply, she told herself that jealousy had nothing to do with it. Her reaction was due to anxiety about her friend, nothing more.

Barbie was falling in love with Denny; all the signs pointed to it. It had been a long time since a man's arms had held her, and on her own admission she was emerging from the frozen emotional state that had followed Toby's death. She was ready to fall in love again. The tragedy of it was, it had been Denny Fox who had happened along at such a momentous point in her life. Why couldn't Alan have been the man to waken her sleeping emotions!

Watching Alan's troubled eyes rake the dance area, Jet pulled herself together sharply, her tone brisk as she suggested, 'Cut in at the end of this dance. Barbie won't give a damn if you're not Fred Astaire! I think I can guess how you're beginning to feel for her, and she's worth putting up a fight for—so go to it, buster!'

She had come here with the sole intention of warning Denny off and it was high time she did just that. But Alan needed no further prodding, because the truants returned to the table then and Barbie, flushed and delectably pretty, fanned her hot cheeks and puffed, 'I'm whacked!'

'Not too whacked to dance with me?' Alan shot to his feet, his eyes holding a pleading expression that made Jet wince with anger for what Denny was doing.

'What do you think?' Barbie sparkled, slipping into his arms, and Jet followed them with her eyes, seeing the almost comically bemused expression on Alan's face and the way he held her, as if she were a fragile piece of porcelain that might break under his tough farmer's hands.

'Your secretary's a charming girl.' Denny had seated himself opposite, leaning back, his face in shadow, out of reach of the light from the candle that burned on the table between them.

'And too nice for you to fool around with!' Jet delivered the words like a spitting cat. He had given her precisely the opening she needed and she was in there, no holding back. 'Keep away from her. She's vulnerable.'

'Jealous, Jet?'

'You've got to be out of your tiny mind!' She sensed rather than saw his laconic shrug and added bitingly, 'I'm fond of Barbie and I won't stand by and see her chewed up and spat out. I won't see her go through what I went through.'

'Bring on the violins!' he said nastily. 'But what's more to the point,' he leaned forward and the flickering candleglow gave his tautly carved features a harshly-drawn masculine beauty, 'mind your own damn business. Barbie's a grown woman; she doesn't need a keeper. Now——' the contempt drained from his voice, replaced by a chillingly polite indifference, 'more coffee? Or would you like to dance?'

'I've had as much coffee as I can take and I don't dance with rats.' The words were out before she could think and she knew she'd made a bad mistake when she saw his mouth tighten. His hand snaked across the narrow expanse of white linen, clasping round her slender wrist, jerking her to her feet.

Short of making a public spectacle of herself there was nothing she could do to prevent him steering her on to the dance floor. In his arms she moved stiffly, holding herself protectively away from the menace of his lithely moving body.

'Why don't you leave me alone?' she asked in a bitter desperation as his thighs brushed hers, weakening her in a way she found shaming.

'I'll never do that—you'd better believe me.' His hand

tightened, pulling her closer, his breath warm on her cheek, his voice low but harsh. 'You've haunted me for six years. Now it's my turn. I've waited for this opportunity for too long to let it slip away. I want you to learn how it feels to be driven half crazy.'

She tried to assimilate this as they danced in silence. She couldn't make sense out of what he'd said. He frightened her. The intensity of his loathing scared her silly. Maybe he was mad—truly insane! The thought made her mind reel, because she didn't know what she'd ever done to make him feel this way.

But it was difficult to think with any degree of clarity when she was being forced into vital awareness of every movement of his body—the brushing of their thighs, the way he held her so close to him, touching him from her breasts down to her hips, their mingled body-heat, the erotic movement of flesh on flesh, creating an intimacy that was painful in its intensity.

Her face hot, she felt the shameful response of her own body to his—the swelling of her breasts, the clenching of her stomach muscles, the quickening of her breath as she tried in vain to quench the quick hot fire of desire that flared to life within her.

She disgusted herself. She knew him, she knew what he was, and yet her body responded to him with a mindless urgency that no amount of common sense, hindsight or simple old-fashioned pride could quell.

Making one last gallant effort to control a rapidly degenerating situation, she fought the crazy desire to press even closer to him and stated, 'If you don't stay away from Barbie I shall be forced to tell her how you treated me. I don't want to—it's not something I'm proud of—but I will if I have to.'

'I shouldn't if I were you.' The lazily arrogant words cut across her angry hiss. 'As it is, Barbie admires you.

You wouldn't want her illusions shattered, would you? What is it with you, anyway? Can't you stand to see another woman getting a little attention?'

She pulled away from him then, pushing through the other couples on the dance floor, finding the ladies' rest room, glad of the quietness that allowed her to get her raging emotions back under some kind of control.

The man was dangerous. An arrogant, lying, cheating womaniser—and crazy, too!

He had no intention of staying away from Barbie, not until he'd grown tired of her. And in the meantime he was carrying on some sick game of his own. He'd talked of retribution, and tonight he'd talked of haunting her— he had to be out of his mind! He was not the same man as the Denny she had once loved so totally.

She sat down on a satin-covered stool in front of the mirror and automatically patted her hair into place, her eyes dark and shadowed. She would have to tell Barbie the truth, and pray that the cheerful redhead's good sense would take over from there. She couldn't stand by and see her get hurt without doing something to try to prevent it.

'So there you are!' The cheerful redhead in question breezed right into the room. 'We've been having one last drink and wondering where you'd got to.'

Barbie plopped down on the stool beside Jet's and looked at her with her head on one side.

'I can't remember when I last had such a good time, can you? The pair of us have lived like nuns for too long. But, like all good things . . . The men are already making noises about getting home. I didn't realise it was gone two until Alan said he'd be doing the milking in four hours' time.'

'Heavens! Then we'd better get a move on!' Jet affected surprise, although she privately felt as if the evening had lasted a year. Smoothing down the silky

fabric of her dress where it clung to her hips, she was
rendered speechless with dismay when Barbie trotted out
of the door in front of her, saying blithely, 'Alan's taking
me back to his place so I can stay overnight and have the
day there with Ben tomorrow. I told him you wouldn't
mind,' she giggled tipsily, "cos Sunday's my day off,
anyway. So Denny's taking you home to save Alan
making the detour. Okay?'

## CHAPTER SIX

THE tension inside the car was oppressive. Denny drove the black Porsche at a speed that played havoc with Jet's already tightly strung nerves. But he handled it well, she had to give him that. He had told her that he liked fast cars, so that was one thing he hadn't lied about!

As they took the road out of Tipper's Batch, heading further into the hills, the headlights cut a golden tunnel through the darkness, the hedgerows drawing in more closely, black, overhanging shapes that increased the feeling of being isolated with him.

He hadn't spoken a word during the drive, and Jet had kept her head firmly averted, staring out into dark nothingness, her hands clenched into fists in her lap. And when his voice came tersely, 'Lost your tongue?' she flinched as though he'd prodded her with a pin.

'Hasn't anyone ever told you it's bad manners to sulk? Surely you don't begrudge Barbie a day away from you?' he added smoothly, and Jet unclamped her jaws just enough to counter,

'Who's sulking? You haven't exactly been bending my ears with pleasant chit-chat. We don't have anything to say to each other, anyway.'

He ignored that, also her cold suggestion that he drop her off at the turning to Foundlands. Swinging the car effortlessly on to the track, he rasped, 'Did you finally give lover-boy the push? Is that why he's making a play for Barbie? Or are you piqued because he's had the plain good sense to drop you for her?'

'You don't know what you're talking about,' she shot

back, then, her mouth curving in a slow smile as a thought occured to her, 'maybe you're the one who's piqued. You've been flirting with her all evening, yet she's gone home with Alan. So what went wrong? Losing your touch? Don't they fall so easily these days?'

She made a clicking sound with her tongue, feeling light-headed and reckless as the car pulled to a halt in front of the house.

'How are the mighty fallen! It was a very different story six years ago, wasn't it? And how did you manage to off-load Pamela Trent? With your usual callousness, I imagine. But don't tell me; I'm not interested.'

She had her hand on the door catch, expecting some scathing comment in answer to her deliberate taunts. Tossing him a haughty look, she slid out of the car and into the blessedly cool night air, puzzled by his lack of response, by his utter stillness. It wasn't like the man he had become to allow her the last word; it made her feel apprehensive.

Jet slammed the car door shut and hurried to let herself into the house, the skin on the nape of her neck prickling. She half expected him to follow her, to give her a verbal slap-down for the way she'd goaded him, implying his lack of virility. And that wasn't true, heaven knew it wasn't. Her own body responses told her he was more sexually dangerous than he had ever been.

But there was no sound of following footsteps, no sound at all except the soft sighing of the breeze and the lazy hoot of an owl.

The house was quiet, too, and she closed the door behind her, leaning against it, her breath coming in shallow gasps. Her heart began to thud as she waited in the darkness, listening for the sound of the Porsche's engine. She heard nothing, so what was he doing? Sitting in the parked car, watching, waiting? Her nerve ends pricked in mute warning.

Suddenly the door behind her moved violently, thrusting her forwards, and she scrambled round, hurling her weight against it, cursing herself for a fool. Her fingers scrabbled for the bolt—why in the name of heaven hadn't she locked the door?

'Aren't you going to invite me in for coffee?'

He was in there with her, the door wrenched effortlessly wide against her puny endeavours, his dark bulk filling the frame. She fumbled for the light switch, flicking it on and her mouth was dry, compressed in a tight line as she snapped, 'Get lost!'

'Manners, manners!' He shook his head slowly in a parody of pained disapproval. But his golden eyes were hard, assessing her, stripping away the sophisticated veneer. 'But what can one expect—with your background? "Dragged up", they told me in the village. "Left to run wild, stop out all night as soon as blink". And not averse to spending the night in the hay with the first man to happen along,' he added savagely.

He turned on his heel, heading for the kitchen, and Jet heard the tap running, the clink of kettle lid, the rattle of cups.

Of all the damned nerve! He was loathsome! Vile! Not content with seducing her, making passionate promises he had no intention of keeping, he had sneaked round the village asking sly questions, digging the dirt. That there hadn't been any dirt to dig; that her story had been one of unloving neglect, she had no intention of stating. She'd see him rot in hell before she tried to justify herself to him! And she'd see him out of her kitchen first!

The fine heels of her strappy evening sandals beat an angry tattoo as she stalked down the passage, and her face was flushed with fury, her eyes huge and jewel-bright as she flung the kitchen door open and cried, 'If you're not out of here in one minute flat, mister, I'm phoning the police!'

'Have some coffee and be quiet,' he said in a bored voice, his back to her. 'Why the hysterics, anyway? What are you frightened of?'

You! she agonised silently, the single word beating against her brain. But she wouldn't give him the satisfaction of knowing that. He was too much, and he was close, and just being in the same room as him, breathing the same air, reminded her of things she had to forget.

Appraising the sleek, powerful body, the hard handsome face he suddenly turned in her direction, she was forced to acknowledge the untenable longings he awoke in her, longings she'd believed she had put aside years ago.

He had removed his tie and his shirt was open at the neck, revealing the beginnings of the crisp golden hair she knew arrowed down his chest. She wanted to touch, and was far more afraid of herself now than she was of him.

Denny poured coffee for them both then removed his jacket, tossing it over the back of a chair and Jet said harshly, 'Don't make yourself too comfortable; you're not staying.'

His hard mouth smiled at her. 'I'll go when I'm ready.'

'Why?' Her vivid eyes darkened and her voice sounded thick. 'Why come here at all? You know what I think of you, and you've made it very clear that you hate the sight of me.'

'I hate what you are,' he came back quickly. 'But I find the *sight* of you very provocative.'

All at once the sexual tension was thick enough to block the air to her lungs. His long, amber eyes undressed her, his mouth softening to a sensual curve. Jet moved restlessly, her heart thudding with primeval warning as she gasped, 'You don't know what I am! You don't know me!'

'Oh, I know you, Jet.' He took a step towards her and her face whitened with the shock of the long-forgotten physical need he was reawakening by his very nearness. 'I've made it my business to know you. And even if I hadn't been able to piece the jig-saw together myself— which I did—I had it from the horse's mouth. Your uncle was very explicit.'

He moved in closer, a pulse throbbing wildly at his temple, the lines of his face harsh. 'One way or another, I know you as well as I know myself.'

Jet backed way, appalled by what she saw in his face, her eyes wide, the pupils dilated until they showed only a thin rim of brilliant sapphire. His hands moved to grasp the soft flesh of her upper arms in a grip that hurt and he jerked her towards him, his voice a soft whisper of menace, 'So let's put my theory to the test, shall we?'

His head came down before she could move, his mouth bruising hers with brutal possession. As his lips plundered hers she could hear his ragged breathing and she twisted frantically, trying to beat him off. But he dragged her closer, so that she could feel the heavy pounding of his heart. Slowly, he deepened the kiss, his mouth seducing hers now instead of giving punishment, his lips moving sensually, parting hers, his hands playing with caressing expertise along the length of her back and buttocks.

Jet's groan of protest died in her throat as his caressing exploration brought a trembling weakness to her body, melting her bones, igniting her senses in a blaze of wanting.

This can't be happening, she thought fuzzily. Six years ago he had held her in his arms and her flesh had melted at his touch, and the magic was still the same, and she couldn't fight it.

'No . . . Please, no . . .' Her words came out huskily as she battled to hold on to the last shrinking remnant of self-control, tears trickling beneath her eyelids as his coaxing lips played with her mouth and then began a lazy, tasting assault on her jawline, sliding down the length of her throat.

Dimly she was aware of his hands on her back, moving the zipper of her dress, but he had awakened a need too great for her cry of protest to be more than a muffled moan in her throat.

The dress slithered to the floor and his fever-bright eyes raked over her body, clad only in scraps of pale silk and lace. She trembled unrestrainedly, her breath caught in her throat, as his hand curved round one breast, pushing aside the nonsense of silky lace, his long supple fingers moving with devastating expertise over the hardening tip. Years of suppression, of icy self-discipline, faded to nothing as his fox-shadow head lowered, as his lips took possession.

Despite knowing she was retreading the path to self-destruction, she twined her fingers in his thick hair, feeling the hardness of bone beneath, and her submission to his domination was implicit in the way her quickened breathing matched his, the arch of her body as she moved forward, closer to him, her mind lost now in a blind vortex of wanting.

'Oh, Denny . . . Denny . . .' Her husky murmur seemed to belong to another woman, wrenched out of past memory, belonging to another time, another place. The instinctive longings that surfaced so strongly now were sharply poignant echoes of that mystically beautiful time when she had first lain in his arms, clung to him, loved him . . .

Her hands clung again now, entreating, without shame as he slowly removed the last wisp of lacy covering, his eyes, intent on her naked body, a bitter-sweet reminder of the way he had looked when she'd offered her body to him before.

She wanted him. The dull ache of unsatisfied need tormented her. She could no longer deny it—no longer wanted to. Her hands moved in a gesture of supplication, her eyes hazed with desire as he stood back, holding her at arm's length while his eyes devoured the slim grace of her body.

'Denny . . .'

'Bitch!' His eyes drifted up and locked with hers and her own widened with shock as she recognised the bitter hatred in the slitted yellow depths.

He moved his hands as if contact with her flesh disgusted him, and turned away, reaching for his jacket.

'So I proved my point,' he bit out. 'You're anybody's, aren't you? I could have taken you just like that!' He snapped derisive fingers under her nose. 'You were begging for it—regardless of the way you know I feel about you. You disgust me! But I'll be back. Don't look to me if you're looking for peace.'

He sauntered to the door, his jacket hooked over his shoulder.

'You pretended I was the first with you, but what about those other poor devils—God help them! You must have teased them half out of their minds. So now you know what it feels like, don't you? It's a lesson someone ought to have taught you long ago. Salutary, was it?'

Jet felt ill, emotionally battered, so ashamed of herself she wanted to curl up and die. Shuddering with self-loathing, she stood in the kitchen until she heard the quick slam of the car door then the muted roar of the Porshe's engine.

Then with shaking fingers she picked up her scattered clothes, hugging them to her as she stumbled up the stairs. The hot bath she took, the vigorous towelling afterwards, did nothing to erase the memory of the touch of Denny's hands.

Normal female desires, suppressed for years behind the ice-cold barrier she had constructed, had suddenly erupted with a violence that appalled her. In her youthful innocence she had given herself to him gladly, and tonight, maturer, tougher, supposedly wiser, she would have again given herself to the man who hated her, humiliated her, haunted her.

She still wanted him, and only him.

Still shaking, Jet crawled into bed, curling up and pulling the covers over her head, trying to blot out the pain. But the pain wasn't outside; it was here, inside her, and would never completely go away because she knew she still wanted him. In spite of knowing the type of man he was, she wanted him. Without comprehending it, she had been faithful to him for six years, in her fashion.

The cool, self-assured mask was back in place the next morning. Jet worked sporadically all day, not pleased with the small amount of progress she was making on her new book, and she was more than relieved when the banging of car doors and the sound of voices told her that Alan had brought Barbie and Ben home.

Ben was clinging to Alan's hand, jigging up and down, chattering like a flock of starlings, his round face flushed with sun and excitement. Barbie hovered in the hall clutching the green chiffon dress. She was wearing one of Alan's shirts, far too big for her, and a pair of his jeans with the legs rolled up.

'I'm the world's biggest fool!' she grinned. 'When Alan suggested I go back with him I didn't think. Must have been the booze! Can you imagine me trotting round the farm, riding on the tractor, feeding the pigs—in all my glam!'

'So I lent her some of my gear. If I hadn't she'd have made me bring her back at dawn. Pity—I rather fancied her in that dress.' Alan's eyes were warm and loving, Barbie's clownish appearance in no way putting him off.

'I'm going to learn to drive the tractor, and the combine, when my legs grow long enough. Aren't I, Alan? Aren't I?' Ben swung on Alan's hand, demanding his share of attention, and Alan rumpled his tousled head.

'Sure you are. Now why don't you run along and have your bath, like your mother said? You need to get an early night, ready for school tomorrow.'

Ben pulled a face but he went willingly enough, his feet sounding like machine gun fire on the stairs, and Jet knew deep relief at having them back home. She felt safer, less afraid of her own raw emotions, with the noisy normality that always surrounded Ben and Barbie.

'I'd better go and get out of these togs and see Ben doesn't drown himself or flood the bathroom.'

Barbie's eyes slid sideways to Alan and Jet said quickly, 'I'll make supper. You'll stay Alan?'

Later, as Jet slid a pizza into the oven, Alan said, 'I want to marry Barbie. Would you mind?'

'Why the heck should I?'

Jet straightened up, smiling at him, amused and slightly amazed that he should have come out with it this way. He was red to his ears, and to spare his embarrassment she turned to the drainer and started to wash the salad, shaking her head when he mumbled, 'I asked you once. I carried a torch for you for years. You're something special to me, Jet.'

'We're special to each other, we both know that.' She turned to him, patting the side of his face with a wet hand, grinning as he screwed up his eyes as droplets of water ran down his neck, trying to make light of what could be a heavy moment for him.

He was affectionate and loyal and probably felt, in some obscure way, that in wanting to marry Barbie he was letting her down, withdrawing the unpossessive support he'd offered over the years.

'And we both know why you offered to marry me. You were sorry for me and generous enough to want to take care of me. Fortunately, I had the sense to say no. It would have been a terrible mistake, because sooner or later you'd have woken up to the fact that there was something missing. I think Barbie's right for you,' she said quickly, guessing he was about to dispute what she'd said about his offer of marriage being rooted in pity. 'Have you said anything to her yet?'

'It's too soon. I know how I feel, but it's too soon for her.' He sat on a kitchen stool watching while she sliced a red pepper and tossed it into the glass salad bowl. 'She enjoys my company and Ben and I get on well together, so there's no problem there. But——' he lifted his wide shoulders in a hopeless shrug, 'there's Denny Fox.'

'What about him?' Jet reached for a granary loaf and hacked chunks off it, her face severe. 'What's he got to do with anything?'

'Last night, watching them dancing, I could see he fancied her, and I'm not up to that kind of competition.'

'Put him out of your mind.' She saw the doubt in his eyes and advised quickly, 'See as much of Barbie as you can. She loves Ben and he loves visiting your place— you've got the advantage there, and it's a big one. Don't

# Say **Yes** to
# romance

# Say yes to free gifts worth over $20.00

**Say YES** to a rendezvous with romance, and you'll get 4 classic love stories—FREE! You'll get an LCD digital quartz watch—FREE! You'll get a stylish ballpoint pen—FREE! And you'll get a delightful surprise—FREE! These gifts carry a total value of over $20.00—but you can have them without spending even a penny!

## MONEY-SAVING HOME DELIVERY!

**Say YES** to Harlequin's Home Reader Service and you'll enjoy the convenience of previewing 8 brand new books every month, delivered right to your home before they appear in stores. Each book is yours for only $1.99—26¢ less than the retail price, and there is no extra charge for postage and handling.

## SPECIAL EXTRAS—FREE!

You'll get our newsletter, *heart to heart*, packed with news of your favorite authors and upcoming books—FREE! You'll also get additional free gifts from time to time as a token of our appreciation for being a home subscriber.

**Say yes** to a Harlequin love affair. Complete, detach and mail your Free Offer Card today!

In August
Harlequin celebrates

# *The* *1000*th
# *Presents*

## Passionate Relationship

by
Penny Jordan

**Harlequin Presents,
still and always the No. 1 romance
series in the world!**

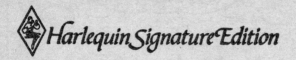

# Carole Mortimer

## *Merlyn's Magic*

She came to him from out of the storm and was drawn into his yearning arms—the tempestuous night held a magic all its own.

You've enjoyed Carole Mortimer's Harlequin Presents stories, and her previous bestseller, *Gypsy*.

Now, don't miss her latest, most exciting bestseller, *Merlyn's Magic*!

## IN JULY

MERMG

### *FREE-digital watch and matching pen*

You'll love your new LCD quartz digital watch with its genuine leather strap. And the slim matching pen is perfect for writing that special person. Both are yours FREE as our gift of love.

# Harlequin HOME READER SERVICE®

## ❧ FREE OFFER CARD ❧

**4 FREE BOOKS**                    **FREE PEN**

Place YES
sticker here

**FREE WATCH**                    **FREE SURPRISE**

Please send me 4 Harlequin Presents novels, free, along with my free watch, pen and surprise gift as explained on the opposite page.          108 CIP CAMD

Name_____
                    (PLEASE PRINT)
Address_____Apt___

City_____

State_____Zip_____

RUSH: FREE GIFTS DEPT.

## BUSINESS REPLY CARD

First Class    Permit No. 717    Buffalo, NY

Postage will be paid by addressee

*Harlequin Reader Service* ®
901 Fuhrmann Blvd.,
P.O. Box 1394
Buffalo, NY 14240-9963

NO POSTAGE
NECESSARY
IF MAILED
IN THE
UNITED STATES

give Denny the chance to get near her.' Her knuckles gripped the bread knife. 'You're worth a dozen of him, and she's a fool if she can't see that!'

'You aiming to feed an army?' asked Alan wryly, his confidence restored by her hot defence and sound advice.

Jet stared at the mound of bread she'd cut, letting out a long, slow breath. Just to think of Denny, let alone discuss him, got her so uptight she hardly knew what she was doing.

'It looks rather like it,' she agreed ruefully, glancing up towards the ceiling where the thumps and squeals which were part and parcel of what Barbie termed The-Ben-Going-To-Bed-Trauma could be heard.

'Move it, buster!' she told Alan. 'Get your elbows off the table and help me lay it. Barbie will be down any minute now, exhausted if I know Ben, and after we've eaten you can invite her to take a lazy evening stroll.'

'Nice thinking. Whatever would I do without you?' He complied good-humouredly, dropping a kiss on the end of her nose, and Jet shrugged.

'I quite fancy myself as an agony-aunt. It gives one a sense of emotional superiority!'

'Cut it out,' Alan grinned, giving her backside a friendly whack. 'Just because you're immune to that old devil, Cupid.'

Immune! Jet felt the now all-too-familiar knife thrust of pain inside her and could have wept. But she fixed a bright smile on her face and threw a scarlet and white checked cloth over the pine table while Alan grabbed a handful of cutlery from a unit drawer, whistling through his teeth.

The pizza was just coming out of the oven when Barbie drifted in. She looked fresh and trim in a mint-green cotton dress, not at all exhausted this evening by Ben's rompings.

'I'm famished!' Her big brown eyes smiled approval at the food on the table and Jet, slicing the pizza, said, 'Dive in, folks.' Her smile was wiped clean off her face when Denny walked through the door.

'Sorry to barge in like this,' he apologised smoothly, and Jet knew he wasn't at all as his hard eyes held hers, probing her soul. 'I came to collect my tie,' he added silkily.

'Tie?' Barbie echoed, lifting puzzled eyes to Jet, turning them back on Denny. 'What tie?'

'I left it here last night. Remember, Jet?' His face was pleasantly bland, the dancing golden lights in his long eyes betraying his amusement.

Jet slewed round quickly and reached for the bottle of white wine she'd put in the fridge to chill, snapping dismissively, 'You must have left it somewhere else. It isn't here.'

'But I put my jacket over the back of that chair,' he countered with deceptively mild innocence. 'So the tie must be somewhere around—though I can't recall exactly where I dropped it. I had other things on my mind at the time.' His smile was tigerish, gloating, deadly, and Jet's hand tightened round the neck of the bottle she was holding. She wished she had what it took to break it over his head! He was going out of his way to imply there'd been some kind of orgy here last night! Was there no end to his need to humiliate her?

As he poked around behind the furniture, Jet knew he was enjoying every minute of this. She saw Alan's raised eyebrows, Barbie's questioning eyes, and knew they believed what he'd set out to make them believe—that the two of them had had a very intimate late-night party here last night.

Her cheeks flooded with bright colour as she remembered just how intimate they had been and how his

calculatedly brutal rejection of her had shamed her. Hadn't he humiliated her enough last night, without putting on this charade? Her insides curled with further humiliation as she realised that her violent blush would have only added the final touches of veracity to his degrading implications.

She felt ill and old and cheap, and when Barbie said, 'It doesn't look as if it's here, but won't you stay and have something to eat?' she had the strong urge to scream and tear her hair out by the roots.

'No thanks, Barbie.' His smile was sweet, honey on the face of the tiger, then, giving Jet a look that told he knew just how much he troubled her, he continued, 'I spent the afternoon with friends of mine at Withington Manor— Arthur and Molly Trent. And Molly always insists on those lavish old-fashioned Sunday teas. Pamela's back home for a time, by the way,' he imparted conversationally, his eyes on Jet. 'You remember her? Exquisite girl.'

He sat down. He didn't want to eat but he wasn't going away, thought Jet sourly. He accepted the glass of wine Alan handed him, raising it, his eyes still intent on Jet.

'Pam and I spent a delightful hour or so reliving old times.'

'I'll just bet you did!' said Jet acidly, then wished she'd held her tongue because Barbie gave her a very strange look and Denny was openly grinning. She didn't want to amuse him, not in any context!

She put her cutlery down; the food was choking her. Not content with humiliating her at every turn, he was carrying on a flirtation with Barbie and hanging around Pamela Trent, too. Was Pamela as eager as she had been to fall into his arms again? Seeing the curved sleek smile on his handsome face, Jet had the distinct impression that she was.

# CHAPTER SEVEN

JET walked slowly up the track, the thin cotton of her shirt sticking to her. This summer had to be heading for some kind of record: no rain in nine weeks and no sign of any change in the hot, heavy weather. Already the land had an arid appearance, burned dry by the brassy sun, and tempers were fraying.

Not that frayed tempers could be blamed entirely on the sun, she admitted wryly. Six weeks had gone by since Denny had sauntered away from Foundlands after planting a completely erroneous impression of their relationship in Barbie's and Alan's minds.

Six weeks, and no one had seen him or heard of him in that time. Tipper's Hollow was empty and locked. Denny, presumably, was back in London, immersed in his work. His absence should have given Jet a much needed sense of relief. Should have done, but didn't. Just knowing that he would eventually return, that he could appear at almost any time of the day or night, gave another subtle but definite twist to the screw of growing tension.

She forced herself to write each day, but her output was way down, the quality of the work she did produce below par in her worried estimation. The sharp, incisive quality of her writing had become blurred and her characters lacked the vigorous, sometimes shocking life that had been one of the hallmarks of her books. And unfortunately, although perhaps inevitably, her edginess had infected those around her.

The only time Barbie had referred to Denny's

implications had been one evening over five weeks ago when Jet had been ironing and Barbie had been curled up in the armchair across the kitchen, a pile of mending on her lap. Normally there would have been a companionable ebb and flow of conversation between them, but the uneasy silence had only been broken by Barbie's taut question, 'What is it with you and Denny Fox?'

Her words made Jet's stomach tighten and she felt sickened by the turmoil the mere sound of his name could produce.

'How do you mean?' she had countered, her expression carefully uninterested, betraying nothing of what she was feeling inside. She had folded one of Ben's school shirts.

Barbie had said tightly, 'Don't try to kid me. There's something wrong, and if you can't tell me, who can you tell? Just lately you've looked, well—haunted—that's the only way I can put it, and it's my guess it's got something to do with Denny Fox.'

Jet's mouth had gone dry; Barbie had more insight than she had given her credit for. He did haunt her. He had said he would, and he did.

'I can't put my finger on it,' Barbie had continued, her head bent over the sock she was darning, her expression hidden. 'But whenever the two of you are together there's a tension you can almost see. It's as if there's something between you other people can't understand.'

And there was, Jet had thought dully, there was indeed. Something dark and tormented, a tightly twisted skein that caught them together in a bitter bonding that had no place in the normality of ordinary human relationships. Denny had never said a truer word when he'd told her that what was between them was private and sick.

'Sometimes it seems as if you actually hate each other,' Barbie had put into the thick silence. 'And yet, from

what he let drop, the two of you were pretty matey the other night.'

This had been said with an acidity that had left Jet in no doubt that Barbie was jealous. But if Barbie believed that Jet and Denny had spent the night together, then that in itself would be enough to warn the redhead off, surely?

There would be no need for Jet to break the silence of years and explain how Denny had used her. All she had to do was maintain a non-committal silence and let Barbie draw her own conclusions.

And she must have done. The change in her friend over the following weeks had implied that much. The former cheerful friendliness seemed gone for ever, replaced by a politeness that bordered on being painful, by a coldness that gave Jet goose bumps.

Even Ben had been tainted by the strained atmosphere between the two adults. School had ended for the long summer holiday and, missing the newly found companionship of children his own age, he had become fractious, sullen and often downright disobedient. 'More trouble than he's worth!' as Barbie had uncharacteristically exploded on one occasion.

Denny was a devious bastard! Jet thought savagely as she drew near the house. He had gone out of his way to charm Barbie, then had calmly informed her, or as good as, that he and Jet were lovers. Then he'd simply disappeared, no doubt gloating over the way he'd driven a wedge between the two friends. He was determined to take the revenge he'd spoken of in any way that presented itself, his hatred running so deep that he didn't care who got hurt besides Jet.

It couldn't go on. She wouldn't let it go on. Unconsciously, she squared her shoulders. Denny was trying to pull her life to pieces for some inexplicable

reason of his own, and she damned well wasn't going to let him! She valued Barbie's friendship and trust, and if telling her the whole sordid truth was the only way of getting it back, then she'd do it. And if the only way to regain her peace of mind, her ability to do her job properly, was to sell Foundlands and move right away, then she'd do that, too!

As she passed inside the front door, welcoming the slightly cooler air, she could hear the rapid tapping of Barbie's typewriter coming from the sitting room where she had her desk.

Jet went on through to the kichen to make coffee, admiring the way Barbie's fingers fled unerringly over the keys. She would be re-typing the first draft of the chapter Jet had completed yesterday, making it easier to reappraise. Jet's typing was atrocious, marred by errors, heavy lines where she'd scored whole passages out, handwritten insertions.

The kettle boiled. Jet poured water on to instant coffee and a sudden clear vision of herself, patiently tapping away with two fingers on the temperamental old portable which had been the best she could afford when she'd started writing, flashed into her head. The clarity of the vision made it seem more real to her than the homelike yet expensively equipped farmhouse kitchen.

She had typed the finished drafts of those first short stories with her heart in her mouth, worried in case the clacking of the keys woke Tod, asleep in the next room behind a dividing wall that was almost paper thin.

Jet screwed her eyes tightly shut, drawing in a harsh breath through pinched nostrils as pain filled her. Tod was gone, and she'd taught herself never to think back to those days when all the love she had had been poured out on the chubby baby boy whose eyes had been as golden as his father's . . .

She shook her head in a violent physical denial of memories too painful to be borne, memories she'd blocked out and had no intention of admitting again. But her hands shook as she put the coffee mugs and a plate of biscuits on a tray, and her face was white under the tan she'd acquired on her walks in the hills as she carried the tray through.

Barbie was sitting at her desk, reading through a typewritten page, engrossed. She looked round with a start when she heard the snick of the door latch as Jet closed it behind her with her foot.

'Coffee,' Jet annnounced brightly, determined to break through the barrier between them. 'I thought I'd have mine with you. How's it going?'

'There are a couple of letters for you to sign,' replied Barbie stiltedly, 'and I've almost typed up to as far as you've got.'

'Fine, thanks.'

Jet took her mug to a deep armchair, sprawling out, relaxing in the sun-scented air which drifted lazily in through the open window. She wished she could detect some thaw in Barbie's attitude, and she frowned slightly when the other girl put down the typewritten sheet she had been checking to ask tersely, 'Why don't you ever put any romance in your books?'

'I do,' answered Jet warily, the question taking her unawares. 'There's a scene at the beginning of chapter two and another in the middle of four. You must have just typed that one.'

'That's not romance,' Barbie argued scornfully. She leaned over and took her coffee from the tray, cradling the mug in her hands, not looking at Jet. 'That's sex. Your heroes treat their women like dirt. Is that how you see men?'

Jet didn't want to go into that, not right now, off the

top of her head. If she came to the point of confiding in
Barbie and told her precisely how she had learned how
men treated women—some men, some women—she
would need time to find the right words, to compose
herself, to convince herself that the painful baring of her
soul would have some value. And here and now, with
barely veiled hostility threatening to pull their relationship apart, wasn't the right moment.

'The books are written mainly for male consumption.'
Jet achieved a light tone. 'And the men who read them
are looking for fast-paced, sexy crime stories, a liberal
dose of tough adventure and hard-bitten macho heroes—
the type of man they'd like to believe they could be if only
they didn't have the mortgage to pay, the kids to raise.
There's no room left in my books for a mush of messy
emotionalism—it would only slow the pace down.'

'If you say so.' Barbie sounded unconvinced, and
although Jet had sounded flippant she felt a cold
heaviness crawl through her veins. She had learned the
hard way that love was a killing emotion. There was no
place for it in her life, no place for it in her books—and
her books were her life now.

The short stories she'd written and sold at the
beginning of her career had been woven around romantic
love. After Tod's birth she had taken an evening job,
working behind a bar in a nearby pub while Denise, the
girl she shared the poky flat with, had baby-sat. The
evening job left her free to look after her baby all day
while Denise was out waitressing. The housework was
soon done and Tod, only two months old when she'd first
started writing, had spent most of his time asleep. So
she'd decided to try her hand at writing stories instead of
reading library books to fill the long hours. And in those
days, right up until Tod's death, she had still been a
romantic at heart, albeit a disillusioned one.

She had believed in happy endings, even though
Denny's betrayal still hurt her deeply with a pain that
shrivelled her whenever she thought of him. Because
even though her love for him had been ill-fated it had
given her Tod, and Tod filled her heart with joy. So, she
had reasoned in those days, her love for Denny had had a
type of happy ending.

But life didn't have happy endings; Jet knew that now.
Real life was tough and cruel, and the weak romantics
went to the wall. Every love she'd ever known had been
taken from her—her parents, her lover, her son, even the
dog, Prince. And if she hadn't coldly shut all memory out
she would have gone to the wall, too.

'Did you see Ben while you were out?' Barbie cut into
her uncomfortable thoughts and Jet pushed her way back
to the here and now, shaking her head.

'No—don't tell me he's gone walkabout again!'

Ben's recently acquired and dismaying tendency to
disappear for hours on end nearly drove his mother
frantic and Jet said quickly, sympathy softening her face,
'Why don't you go out and find him then drive him over
to the farm? I know Alan and his mother would be only
too pleased to see you.'

'No.' The emphatic shake of Barbie's head made Jet
wonder, not for the first time, if the couple had fallen out.
Alan's visits to Foundlands had dropped off to nothing.
In fact, Jet recalled, he'd only been here once since he'd
confided that he wanted to marry Barbie. 'Though I will
go out and look for Ben.' The redhead got to her feet, not
looking at Jet as she added stonily, 'I'll finish replying to
your fan mail this afternoon.'

'Barbie—what's wrong?' Jet was on her feet too,
hating the atmosphere that as day followed day seemed
to thicken perceptibly. If something weren't done about
it soon it would become a thick, impenetrable wall.

'Something's getting to you,' she followed on, her vivid blue eyes worried. 'Is it something I've done, or said? Or is it this place?' she added. 'Would you and Ben be happier somewhere less isolated?'

Even as she finished speaking, Jet saw the prickly tension drain out of her friend, watched the bright head droop and then come up again, the brown eyes misty.

'Idiot!' Barbie croaked, close to tears. 'Of course it's nothing you've said or done. And Ben and I love it here, the only fly in that particular ointment being his horrible behaviour just lately.' She turned from Jet and began to shuffle papers on her desk. 'I've got a lot on my mind. It's Alan, you see.'

'Alan?' Jet questioned gently. 'What's he done?'

'Nothing. Everything.' Barbie answered enigmatically, looking as much at sea as Jet felt. 'He hasn't actually said as much, but from the broad hints he dropped the last time I saw him alone, I think he'd like me to marry him.'

'So?' Jet smiled tentatively. 'What's wrong with that? Don't you fancy him? You're not——' her voice iced over, 'you're not still starry-eyed over your "Heavenly Man"—Denny Fox?'

'No way!' Barbie smiled crookedly, her eyes evading Jet's. 'He's strictly for dreaming about; I've always known that. That type of man always is—for girls like me. But I would look for some romance in a marriage, and from what Alan was saying I got the impression that he only wanted a wife because his mother's getting on in years—and I'd want something more.'

'Barbie!' Jet's grin was unrestrained. 'Alan has never been noted for the poetic quality of his speech! And when he's embarrassed, as he probably would have been when he was trying to tell you how he felt, he's practically inarticulate! So if your only worry is that he sees you as a

mother-substitute or an unpaid housekeeper, then forget it!'

'It isn't.' Barbie, her mouth dragged down, didn't join Jet's laughter. 'I've got a few hang-ups of my own. I know now that I don't want to spend the rest of my life on my own. I want my own home, my own man. And Ben needs a father figure—so, would I be marrying Alan because he'd fit that particular role?'

'You must know how you feel about him, whether you really care about him, or not,' Jet pointed out, and Barbie sighed.

'I was beginning to care about him, quite a lot, actually, before he made those oblique references to marriage. But Denny forced me to change my mind.'

'He did?' Jet's eyes narrowed. She might have known that devil would manage to sour things up. 'How? By trying to make love to you?'

'Lord, no! There's never been anything like that between us—I told you. He just happens to be one of the kindest men I've ever known—and by far the best looking. But that doesn't mean I don't have both feet very firmly on the ground as far as he's concerned. No, he told me,' her eyes slid away, fastening on the view from the window, 'or as good as, that you and Alan were lovers. That you were living with him here for some time before Ben and I came down. And I know how you feel about men and marriage, so I thought that if Alan was in love with you but knew you'd never marry him, then I'd be a fool if I let myself care for a man who would always be in love with someone else. Do you see what I mean?' she mumbled drearily.

Jet saw, only too well. She sat down heavily, the anger inside her building up. The swine! The devious, lying swine! No wonder he'd left the district!

Trying to control the rage which demanded the release

of screaming or throwing things around the room—or both, she asked, 'Just when did he drop that pearl of information?'

'That Sunday night. You remember? Ben and I had spent the day with Alan and Denny dropped by, looking for his tie. He came back much later; you'd already gone to bed. I made some coffee and we got talking, and I suppose I must have told him about the way I was starting to feel about Alan—we'd had a lovely walk earlier that evening, and I was feeling gooey, and excited. Anyway, that's when he told me about you and Alan. I don't think I've felt really happy since that weekend. Oh, I know you and Alan go back a long time, and it's none of my business if you slept together, but it certainly made me put the brake on my feelings for him.'

'I'll just bet it did!' Jet retorted hotly, turning the facts over in her mind. No matter who else got hurt in the process, Denny Fox was set on spreading dirt about her. He had admitted that Barbie admired her, so he'd gone all out to put a stop to that. Telling Barbie that she and Alan were lovers only hours after intimating that she and Denny had spent the night together, had been a masterly stroke in the art of reputation-shredding! 'Will it help you to know that Alan and I have never been lovers?' Jet got to her feet, smoothing the fabric of her cotton skirt over her hips. She was seething with a restless energy, the need for positive action very strong. If she could lay her hands on Denny Fox she'd throttle him on the spot!

'Denny hates my guts,' she told Barbie. 'He'd do anything to blacken my name, humiliate me and see any good relationship I've got going shot to hell! Don't ask me why, because I don't know myself. Just believe me. And I suggest you work things out for yourself from there. Alan cares for you, he told me as much himself, and it's up to you to find out if you feel the same way

about him. Why don't you go over and see him this afternoon? I'll find Ben and take him into town so you won't have to worry about him.'

It didn't take long to find Ben. Jet went straight to the stream which flowed behind the house, remembering how the glinting, chattering water had fascinated her as a child. His clothes were wet through, his face streaked with mud, and it took half an hour to get him washed and into clean clothes. She had never permitted herself such close contact with the small boy before, and gentling a comb through his hair, easing the tangles out, brought an uncomfortable lump to her throat, a stinging of tears to her eyes.

As she hustled him down the stairs and through the hall, the sound of the typewriter came clearly. Jet only hoped Barbie wasn't going to glue herself to her desk for the rest of the day, because that meant her offer to take Ben out of the way would be a waste of what she knew would be a real ordeal.

But whether Barbie took advantage of what Jet had offered—time to contact Alan and freedom from the doubts Denny had created regarding her own relationship with him—was her own affair. There was nothing more Jet could do.

Settling Ben in the car, she bit back the rising tide of angry resentment that threatened to overwhelm her when she thought of the lengths Denny would go to in order to serve out doses of the retribution he had spoken about. Brooding about it would do no good. She couldn't go down to his cottage and demand to know what he thought he was playing at, because he wasn't there.

She did all she could to put thoughts of Denny out of her mind. Driving to Tolcaster along the familiar lanes, she tried to talk to Ben. It wasn't easy because their

relationship was cagey—she had purposely kept it that way—and Ben's mind was running on one track—the empty state of his stomach—but his eyes did brighten a little when she promised lunch as soon as they'd found somewhere to park the car, and he demanded, 'Then can we go home again?'

'Later.' She searched her brain to think of something that might interest the child who was uneasy in her company and who would undoubtedly rather be at home, wandering the stream banks and meadows, than in the crowded streets of the market town, and she came up with, 'There's a park we could go to. It's in the grounds of what's left of a castle.'

There was only a crumbling, fenced-off tower and the foundations of walls which had been demolished by Cromwell's troops, but there were slides and swings for the children, a grassy picnic area and a small children's zoo.

'They built the castle here because they could look out over the lowlands and spot the ememy,' Jet told Ben.

They were standing in the shadow of the ruined tower, on the high red sandstone escarpment that overlooked the slow-running looping river and the flat water meadows.

'I want to go on the swings.' Ben wasn't interested in the view or why the castle had been built here seven centuries ago. He licked his ice-cream cone lovingly, and Jet wondered where he put it all—he'd only just consumed a lunch of monumental proportions!

'Well, if you don't think you'll be sick, you can.' She eyed him doubtfully as he crammed the remainder of his cone into his mouth and wiped his hands down the front of his shirt. Even at nearly five years old, his hands still had that starfish quality that Tod's had possessed.

Her heart gave an uncomfortable lurch as she forced herself to answer the boy's wide grin. It wasn't his fault that every time she looked at him she was seeing the ghost of a child who would have been roughly the same age, had he lived.

Taking his hand and trying not to screw her face up when she encountered the warm stickiness of it, she told him, 'We'll take a look at the children's zoo first—give your lunch time to go down. Okay?'

'Okay.' He seemed willing enough to fall in with her plans, and he trotted on chubby tanned legs at her side, placid and sunny-tempered, accepting her without his usual wariness for the first time that day, or any day.

But half-way across the close-cut, sun-dried expanse of grass, Jet felt him stiffen and pull to a standstill. And before she could do anything about it he wrenched his hand free from hers and flew over the turf, screeching, 'Denny! Hey, Denny—wait for us!'

Jet's heart slammed sickeningly then, and her mouth went suddenly dry, her narrowed eyes following the direction of Ben's flying body. There was no mistaking the tall, lithe form, the close-cropped hair—more gold than russet in the harsh sunlight. The woman he was with took a few seconds longer to place; Pamela Trent's looks were starting to blur with the extra weight she'd put on during the past six years, but she was still a beautiful woman, perfectly dressed and poised.

Denny scooped the child up in his arms, laughing, his eyes raking over the other people strolling in the sun. She knew the exact split second when his golden eyes identified her because the laughter was sponged from his face, leaving it hard.

Reluctantly, Jet began to walk towards the man, the woman and the child. Her instinct was to turn and walk away, her head high, but she could hardly abandon Ben!

Her face was coolly composed, but she was shaking inside as she watched Denny turn to Pamela, saying something that apparently amused the other woman, because she was still smiling with her mouth as she turned to watch Jet's unhurried approach with hard eyes, full of dislike.

It took all her willpower to hold on to her self-control, to batten down her surging anger as she drew nearer to the man who would do anything, say anything, in order to humiliate and degrade her.

Having to witness the amusement between those two was all she needed. It turned her stomach! Jet could guess the nature of the private joke. How laughably pathetic she must have seemed six years ago, creeping up to the front door of Withington Manor, pleading to be allowed to speak to Denny, only to be sent away with a flea in her ear, her world in pieces.

Six years ago those two had been engaged. So what had happened? Had Pamela told him that a gypsy-haired brat had come calling, asking for him? Had she found out, then, about the night in the shepherd's hut, her ensuing jealous anger causing a scene that had given Denny the excuse he needed to break the engagement?

Jet couldn't begin to guess, but whatever had happened they looked close enough now, smiling, their heads together, her hand possessively touching his bare, tanned arm. Maybe Pamela had come to terms with his apparent inability to make any emotional commitment and was willing to make herself available whenever he turned those sensual amber eyes in her direction. It would be all too easy to lose one's pride and integrity when faced with the potent sexual magnetism Denny exuded. Jet knew that, to her cost!

Suddenly she didn't feel annoyed by Pamela's superior, smirking smile. She felt sorry for the woman because

she, too, knew how it felt to respond physically to the man who treated his women like dirt. But, unlike Pamela, Jet had no intention of ever letting herself respond again.

'No Barbie?' asked Denny as Jet stepped from the grass to the bordering gravelled path where the others stood. 'She's not sick?'

Jet shook her head, scorning the concern in his eyes. He didn't care who was sick or hurt just so long as all was well with his world.

'She's fine.'

'Me and Jet's having a day out,' Ben informed them as Denny shifted the child's not inconsiderable weight more comfortably against his hip.

'Is that so?' The curl of Denny's lip showed only too well the doubt he felt over any such undertaking on Jet's part, a doubt that was further endorsed when he muttered, his eyes biting hers, 'Who twisted your arm!'

She ignored that. She spoke to Ben, her clear voice light and controlled. 'Time we took a look at the zoo, Ben.'

But the small boy seemed suddenly to have developed a rapid case of acute deafness, and Pamela injected into the silent pause, 'I simply must fly, Denny, sweet. Thanks for lunch—see you very soon, hmmm?' She reached up and placed a softly lingering kiss on the corner of his mouth then turned, her eyes dismissingly cutting through Jet, and walked quickly away.

'So you're still seeing Pamela,' Jet couldn't prevent herself from saying, her voice acid with remembered distaste for the woman who, with a few well-chosen words, had finally shattered her romantic illusions all those years ago. 'It must be one of the longest-running engagements on record.'

'What on earth——' Denny began, his eyes puzzled,

but Jet didn't hear the rest because something heavy hit her in the small of the back, knocking her off balance. She twisted round quickly, then bent to pick up the football that lay at her feet, the soft printed cotton of her light skirt swirling around her long legs. Grinning, she lifted the ball and held it above her head, pausing only for a second before tossing it back to the two abashed looking youths who had obviously been expecting a tongue-lashing for carelessness.

Ben chuckled, wriggling down from Denny's arms, and would have raced off to join the older boys who were now circumspectly dribbling the ball away over the grass.

'Are you all right?' Denny asked quietly, but Jet didn't bother to answer that. What did he care? She caught Ben's hand as he started to run after the boys with the ball.

'No you don't, buster! We're going to look at the animals, remember?'

She laughed at the look of chagrin on his round, freckled face, but her expression straightened when Denny put in, 'Sounds like a good idea. We'll all go.' He held out a hand to Ben, but much to Jet's surprise the child clung to her, looking up at her as they began to walk to the entrance of the small zoo.

'You throw a good ball, Jet,' he said in all seriousness. 'Not like Mom. It goes straight up in the air with her, and mostly lands up behind her.'

'We'll have to hurl a ball around our field some time, won't we?' she offered, wondering at the way something seemed to melt inside her as she felt his grubby little hand hold her own more tightly, wondering that she could bear to welcome the closeness that was suddenly emerging.

She swallowed around the lump in her throat, then stiffened with annoyance as she saw Denny at the

turnstile, paying for their entrance.

'There's no need for you to come along,' she rasped. 'Ben and I were enjoying our day.'

And this was exactly true, she realised, surprised at herself. She had never willingly spent any longer in Ben's company than she needed, because she had been afraid of the painful reminders a developing relationship between them would inevitably provoke. She had had enough of pain in her life without going looking for it, so keeping her distance had seemed like sound policy.

'I'd like to come along,' he answered blandly as he pocketed their tickets. 'I've already broken the journey back to the cottage, so I might as well make a day of it.' His eyes defied her to make a scene in front of the child, but when Ben ran on ahead to a compound housing two Shetland ponies he said tersely, 'What were you sniping at back there? Why shouldn't I see Pam? And what was that about the longest-running engagement on record?'

'Forget it,' snapped Jet, joining Ben at the wire, already sorry she'd mentioned the other woman and the fact that she had been Denny's fiancée and could be still, for all she knew. Every nerve in her body was alert to the danger this man posed to her peace of mind, and it was far from a comfortable feeling. Just to be near him set her pulses hammering, the blood roaring through her veins, every fibre of her being tuned in to the animal magnetism of him. It made her ashamed of herself; she knew the type of man he was, knew that the only thing he had in mind where she was concerned was the need to hurt and humiliate. So why did her wretched body respond to him this way? Was it a hang-over from that time when they'd loved and been happy, or was it more basic than that? Whatever it was she had to fight it.

Losing interest in the ponies, Ben scampered away to peer into an oversized doll's house with a plate glass

front, behind which a dozen or so white mice resided, and Denny said flatly, 'I've read all your Roger Blye books. In fact I'd read all but the latest before I found out they were written by you.'

'You—what?' Jet's feet dragged to a halt. Was there no way to stop this man knifing his way into her life? Her Roger Blye identity had been one of her closest-kept secrets.

'Congratulations.' He turned to face her, his eyes yellow and hard. 'Now I understand how you can afford to live in style. Maybe your lovers don't have to pay quite as highly for your favours as I'd imagined at first.'

'You bastard!' White to the lips, she hated the cool audacity that kept him coldly amused, sneeringly offhand. Was there to be no end to his intrusions, his insults?

'Why?' One brow lifted above contemptuous eyes as he questioned her castigation. 'Don't you like it when someone probes behind that sophisticated exterior to find the real woman beneath? Woman!' his voice jeered. 'Those books could have been written by a man. Is that the way you sublimate your feelings? Is it the only way to make them acceptable—to publish under a man's name? Because you treat the men in your life like your heroes treat their women—brutally, like disposable playthings. You're hard as nails, aren't you, Jet? Brutal, unfeminine. It's not the way you seemed on your eighteenth birthday, but with hindsight I see that was all an act. You were born with iron in your soul.'

She wasn't going to deny any of it, not to him. And he was right about her being hard now, he had made her that way. Her head came up defiantly, her magnificent eyes proud.

'Who told you?'

'No way!' He shook his head slowly, his handsome

male mouth curling in derision. 'Do you think I'd tell you? Let's just say I got my information through slightly devious methods, and I gave my promise I wouldn't reveal the source. Unlike you, I keep my promises.'

Jet could have said plenty to contradict that blatant lie, but Ben came panting back. He'd been all round the exhibits and, according to him, had worked up a terrible thirst.

Watching Denny take Ben to buy a can of Coke from a kiosk selling ices and soft drinks, Jet seethed over his latest insults. First, she was a kept woman, and then she treated her men the way her heroes treated their women! That was a laugh! No man had been allowed near her since Denny had ground her heart under his heel.

He must have had his information from Barbie or Alan; no one else knew about her pen name. She felt no resentment against either one of them; Denny had admitted to using devious methods and she knew, who better, how he could turn on the charm, make a person believe black was white if he put his mind to it.

It was Denny she resented, deeply and bitterly. He had harmed her before when she'd been young and particularly vulnerable, and for some unimaginable reason he was intent on harming her again. It couldn't go on, it had to be stopped—before he drove her out of her mind!

When the Coke was disposed of, the empty can deposited in one of the litter bins, Ben ran ahead to the play area and Jet remarked coldly, 'Your plan didn't work, you know.'

'What plan?' He didn't really sound interested, his eyes were on Ben as he climbed up the steps to the slide.

'Whatever it was you had in mind when you told Barbie that Alan and I were lovers. There's a law against slander.'

'It needed saying.' He shrugged dismissively, and

despite her loathing for him Jet couldn't tear her eyes
from the powerful shoulders under the light fabric of the
short-sleeved dark brown shirt he wore above cream-
coloured snug fitting pants. 'I didn't have to be a genius
to understand the way Barbie was beginning to feel about
Alan. She's a nice kid and she can't have had an easy
time since her husband died, and I didn't want to see her
get hurt. So I let her know, gently, I hope, that you and he
had been shacking up at Foundlands, and that you hadn't
denied it when I referred to him as "lover-boy".'

'It wouldn't occur to you that you might be wrong?'
Hot colour crept along her cheekbones and her hand
itched to slap his hard, egocentric face. He'd put two and
two together and come up with a thousand and still, in his
blind arrogance, thought he'd got the right answer!

'Not where you're concerned, no.' His eyes were hard,
unforgiving. 'I know you inside out. Does it hurt? Does
the pain get sharper every time I probe something nasty
out for public examination? Do you lie awake at nights
and wonder what slimy hidden thing I'm going to pull out
next? Do you, Jet?'

The shrieks and shouts of the children in the play area
faded to nothing under the cruel intensity of his words,
and despite the heat of the brassy sun she shivered, the
tiny hairs on the back of her neck pricking with some
nameless yet insidious terror. Her mouth was parched
and dry, her vivid eyes wide with unhidden distress as
she whispered huskily, knowing she had to get at the
truth, yet afraid of what she might hear, 'You really do
hate me! God, how you hate me!'

'And it's growing all the time,' he conceded tonelessly.
'Remember that, Jet. Remember it every minute of every
hour.'

Her stomach curled at the ferocity of his words and she
ground out desperately, 'Why? I have to know why!'

The deadly purpose she sensed behind the implacable, heart-stopping features was underlined by the burning gold of his eyes as he turned them on her. She knew his mind was on fire with a hatred that threatened to consume them both.

'What have I ever done to you?' Her words held an unconscious pleading, her own bitterness at the way he had used and cheated her now swamped by her need to know.

He had turned abruptly on his heels as if the sight of her disgusted him, and her hand involuntarily grasped his arm, demanding an answer.

The feel of the warm, tanned skin with its covering of fine golden hairs sent alarm signals pricking through her body, signals which converged, humiliatingly, in a sharp ache of desire in the pit of her stomach.

He turned back swiftly, brushing away her detaining hand as if it burned, his breath drawn roughly into his lungs. There were pain lines etched deeply around his cruelly thinned mouth, and his eyes seared her soul as he bit out, 'You killed our child. Perhaps your hard, selfish little mind can't see that being reason enough. But it is in my book. You killed our child, Jet. And I made a promise, on my dead child's life, that I'd find you and make you pay—and go on paying.'

# CHAPTER EIGHT

JET sank thankfully on to one of the many bench seats round the play area as Denny walked away. Her legs were shaking too much to carry her to the swings to bring Ben away.

Besides, she needed time to think, to come to terms with Denny's cruel accusations. Her heart was fluttering wildly, out of control but perfectly in tune with her confused, darting thoughts.

How could he have known about Tod's existence? How could he have known he had a son and not, at the very least, made enquiries about his wellbeing?

Easily, she supposed. Responsibilities and long-term commitments were not his style.

And yet—her chaotic thoughts darted hither and thither, like terrified small animals trapped in a labyrinthine bolthole where every exit was blocked—and yet he had not been acting when he'd shown how much Tod's death had affected him.

The hatred he had for her, and which had completely puzzled her, had been violently and damningly explained when he'd told her of the promise he'd made to make her pay and go on paying.

No one from the village knew she had given birth to a son, so Denny couldn't have picked his information up from there. Alan had known but he had told no one, not even his mother; he had given his word on that and Jet believed him.

So Denny must have read the report of the child's death in the papers. The thought made her feel physically

sick. The gutter press in particular had made a meal of the tragedy, their unsubtle innuendoes about the flighty nature of the dead child's absent, fun-loving mother more damning than if they'd actually laid the blame at her feet.

The twisted, barbed talons of the guilt she had buried deep in her mind broke free of the self-imposed barrier of forgetfulness and wrenched at her savagely. If only she hadn't left Tod in Denise's incompetent hands . . .

Unknowingly, a low groan of despair escaped her ashen lips, but Jet was blind to the curious stare of an elderly woman who pushed a pram along the path in front of her.

'Are you alright, dearie?' The woman sat down, her bulk filling the spare space on the bench, the pram squarely in front of her. 'I think I'll just rest my feet a bit. Hot, isn't it?'

Bright brown eyes peered at Jet from a wrinkled inquisitive face but Jet didn't hear a word as the woman droned on, rocking the pram, 'This is Sara, my first grandchild—isn't she sweet! I often bring her here when the weather's good. Gives our Marge a bit of a break. Mind you, I didn't have anyone to give me a break when my lot were small.'

*I wasn't responsible for his death—I wasn't!* Jet's screaming thoughts blanked out the woman's voice. *God, tell me I wasn't! Denny couldn't be right, could he?*

'Oh! Poor little mite! Did you see the header he took off that swing?' The woman nudged Jet. 'Look, over there, see? His mother's not with him by the look of things. Leastways, no one's picking him up.'

The woman nudged again and Jet practically jumped out of her skin. She stared at the wrinkled old face with blank, withdrawn eyes, not taking in a word that was

said to her until Ben's unmistakable bellows cut through
her tormented thoughts.

She was on her feet immediately, grabbing her
shoulder bag by its strap, flinching as the woman
muttered sourly, stabbing at the raw, newly opened
wound of guilt, 'Some mothers should be locked up! Talk
about being irresponsible!'

Jet's feet pounded the grass and she dropped to her
knees as Ben stumbled towards her, his hands clamped
over his face from whence blood and bellows issued in
equal measure.

Gently but firmly, she eased his hands away from his
face, her other hand scrabbling in her bag for tissues.
Mopping him up, exerting a gentle pressure on the
almost non-existent bridge of his nose to stem the
bleeding, she felt her heart swell with an inrush of the
maternal love she had forgotten she was capable of.

'It's alright, poppet.' She drew him into her arms, tears
welling over as she felt his arms twine chokingly around
her neck, felt his head nuzzle deeply into her shoulder.

Something within her was thawing, loosening, the
formidable barriers she had erected after Tod's death
crumbling apart. After denying the possibility of love
ever reaching her again she was amazed by how easy it
was to admit it to her heart. Easy, and strangely healing
. . .

When his sniffles had died down, she flicked the tears
from her own cheeks and loosened his hands from their
stranglehold around her neck. Grinning crookedly, she
told him, 'We look as if we've been in a fight! Let's go
and get cleaned up, shall we? There's a place I know
where we can get a cup of tea as well.'

Ben gave back a grin that echoed her own, his dirty,
tear-stained face infinitely lovable. Had Denny's words
broken through the barrier she had coldly erected

between herself and Barbie's child? Or had her frozen heart, unknown to her, been ready and willing to give love again?

A strange, weary contentment washed through her as hand in hand they left the castle grounds and walked a few yards down a cobbled street to the castle tearooms. In the washroom they surveyed each other with mutual delight, undecided as to who looked the bigger sight. Jet's hair was coming down, her eyes sparkling above dirt-streaked cheeks, her floral skirt and ice-blue silk blouse grubby and bloodstained. She would put Denny's accusations to the back of her mind for what was left of the day, and she would enjoy Ben's company and hope he enjoyed hers. Tomorrow, when Barbie was back in charge of her son—then she would think about the things Denny said.

After ten minutes' effort with hot water and her comb, Jet pronounced herself reasonably satisfied. 'I don't think they'll actually throw us out now if we ask for some tea, do you? Let's go and see what they've got. Hungry, Ben?'

He was, as always, and settled for egg sandwiches and fruit cake, and while Jet was sipping her tea she said consideringly, 'You know where we parked the car? Well, near the car park there's a pet shop—we passed it on the way up into town. And I noticed some puppies right in the window.'

Her lips twitched as the small boy stared at her, his slice of cake hovering half-way to his mouth.

'And I've been thinking that we ought to have a dog at Foundlands. Only I couldn't see who would have time to look after it. It was silly of me not to think of you——' She smiled at the way he wriggled with excitement, his face growing red as he yelped,

'I'd look after it, Jet! I wouldn't mind!'

'Are you sure?' she enquired with the solemnity she knew he felt the occasion merited. 'You do have plenty of time, especially when you're on holiday from school, I suppose. Of course,' she put her tea cup down neatly on its saucer, 'if you would be willing to take care of a puppy it would have to belong to you, wouldn't it? It would only be fair. Shall we go and take a look at what they've got?'

The black labrador puppy was asleep on Ben's lap when Jet pulled the estate car to a standstill in front of Foundlands. Its rubbery body looked boneless and Ben's arms, cradling it, were protective, his eyes glowing with pride.

'Carry him inside and introduce him to your mother,' she said, knowing Barbie must be home because Alan's Land Rover was parked outside so she wasn't visiting him, as Jet had suggested.

She watched the small boy as he carefully carried the sleeping puppy inside, her eyes soft. The animal would make extra work; Ben was too young to be expected to train him properly. But as long as the boy knew the dog was his, as long as he believed its welfare was entirely in his hands, then Jet had no objection at all to keeping an eye on its feed requirements, mopping up after it until it was house-trained.

Gathering up the new arrival's luggage—the soft collar and lead, feed bowls, puppy foods and the woolly blanket they'd use to line a suitable cardboard box until it grew big enough to need a full-size basket—Jet followed.

The voices coming from the living-room told Jet that Barbie and Alan were very properly admiring Foundlands' new inhabitant. And Jet, burdened down, pushed the door open with her shoulder and froze, her breath dragged out of her body, when she saw that Denny was one of the group of admirers.

What was he doing here? Had he come to elaborate on the bald accusation he'd hurled at her only an hour or two ago?

'Jet—he's super!' Barbie, all smiles, cut into Jet's raging thoughts. 'I didn't know you wanted a dog!'

'He's not mine,' disclaimed Jet, a dreadful weariness of spirit suddenly dragging her down. But her eyes smiled down into Ben's. 'He belongs to your son, and he's the one who's going to have to keep him out of mischief and take him for walks. Hi, Alan, long time no see!'

She ignored Denny, conscious of the way his presence filled the room, making it almost impossible for her to breathe, knowing his eyes were on her all the time, their expression both puzzled and puzzling.

'I'll just take his lordship's baggage through to the kitchen,' she excused herself, and Barbie followed, shaking her head.

'You shouldn't have done it, Jet. Pedigree labradors cost a bomb! But thanks. You've only got to look at Ben to see how he adores it.'

'I thought a dog would be company for him. There was a dog here when I was a child, and he was the only company I had most of the time.' Jet smiled, not letting Barbie see how much remembering Prince could still hurt. 'Perhaps they'll keep each other out of mischief.'

She put the puppy food away in a cupboard and filled one of the plastic feed bowls with water, putting it on the floor, asking tightly, 'What's he doing here?'

'What? Oh——' Barbie bit into her soft lower lip, her brown eyes worried. 'You don't mind, do you? I thought about what you'd said, only I couldn't bring myself to go over—not without being invited. For all I knew he might have had second thoughts after, well, after I sent him away before. So I phoned and somehow or other he invited himself over for supper, and——'

'Of course I don't mind!' Exasperation and amusement jostled for supremacy. 'Alan's always welcome, you know that. I meant *him*. Denny!'

'Oh.' Barbie shrugged. 'I honestly don't know. He just turned up. He walked through the door only seconds before you got back with Ben. I expect he came to see you.'

Jet hoped not. They hadn't long parted company, and he'd given her enough food for thought to last a lifetime. He hated her with an intensity that would inevitably drag him back to her, time after time, to dole out punishment. But not so soon, surely not so soon!

She felt so tired, emotionally exhausted by his relentless pursuit, his driving need to punish her. And she could have wept from sheer tiredness of spirit when he walked into the kitchen.

'Have you got a mop and bucket handy?' His voice was lazily amused but his eyes were hard, pinning Jet down, and she didn't think she could stand much more of it. 'The new member of the family has disgraced himself.'

'I'll go.' Barbie was already filling a bucket at the hot tap, grabbing a floor cloth.

Jet had gone to the sink, too, and she stayed there now, her shoulders rigid, waiting to hear Denny walk out. But she knew by the tension that curled itself inside her that he was still in the room, even though he said nothing, didn't move, as far as she could tell.

She closed her eyes, willing him to go, knowing she couldn't stand much more of his cruel, tormenting game. Only it was far from being a game.

Strangely enough, she didn't loathe him now as she had done, and resentment had no hold on her thoughts, not at this moment. Compassion stirred instead, a deep pitying that his grief over the death of their child had produced the violent hatred that she knew was alien to

the man he had been. He might have been a careless,
unthinking womaniser, but he had also been gentle and
kind, incapable of the hatred that now burned in his soul.

'Ben tells me,' he said at last, 'that you've decided to
call the dog Prince.'

The sound of his voice, breaking the tense silence,
made her shudder weakly. It was carefully controlled,
without inflexion, a remorseless reminder that without
the violence of hatred their relationship was empty, any
conversation between them a mouthing of meaningless
nothings.

'Was that your idea, or his?'

'Mine. Does it matter?' The words came out on a
whisper, a near-silent appeal for him to leave her in
peace. There was so much that needed to be said, so
much that this bitter, brooding man did not understand,
that talk of trivialities, such as the naming of a puppy,
was a superficial irritant she hadn't the strength of mind
to bear with. There was so much to tell him, and yet she
had nothing to say that would alter his slating opinion of
her.

'It matters.' He joined her at the sink, his nearness
disrupting her heartbeats, making the adrenalin flow.
She moved jerkily away, her limbs feeling as if they were
strung on wires. He followed, pushing her firmly into a
chair, pinioning her with his eyes. The amber had
darkened to deepest topaz, the dark, gold-tipped lashes
lowering until he regarded her through glittering
determined slits, holding her immobile with the knowledge that the reality of this confrontation, of any
confrontation between the two of them, was, for her, the
only reality there was.

Everything else was slipping, shifting as though the
foundations of her life had been built on soft sand.

Her ability to work was going, moving inexorably

from her grasp, the heart she'd put into deep freeze after Tod's death was thawing, changing. Only one thing remained constant—the pull, hating or loving, that existed between herself and this quiet, watchful man.

'What happened to your old dog, Prince?' He presented her with the question, his eyes not leaving hers as he swung a kitchen chair around and straddled it, his arms resting along the top of the slatted wooden back.

'Micah shot him.' Jet closed her eyes briefly, her mouth tightening against the pain of remembering. And then, because the old sheepdog was a memory they had in common, even though Denny had not actually seen him, she felt he had the right to know. She told him huskily. 'After—when Micah told me to leave I tried to take Prince with me. He was old and he—Micah, that is—had talked of getting rid of him because he wasn't much good as a working dog. Too old, you see, and going blind. So it wasn't as if I was taking something he valued, or was fond of, was it?'

Her thickly fringed eyes darkened to inky sapphire as she searched his impassive features, her lips trembling as she recalled the shock of witnessing so much spite.

'Prince was about the only friend I had then.' Unconsciously, her voice hardened, became brisker, as she continued, 'I knew if I left him behind he'd have one hell of a miserable time until Micah remembered he'd decided to get rid of him. He used his old .22 Webley, the air rifle he kept for shooting rats and crows.'

'Tell me what happened.' His voice was taut, his narrowed eyes sweeping over the cool purity of her features, questioning with an urgency that Jet, back in time on the rain-lashed track of that long ago blustery autumn day, did not see.

'I'd packed what clothes I had into a plastic carrier and enough food to keep both of us going into another. I

reckoned he owed us that,' she answered heavily,
dragging the words out because she'd never spoken of the
event before. But she knew she had to speak of it now
because, for good or ill, Denny was part of her. 'I'd made
a lead out of binder twine and we were walking away,
down the track, when Micah came after us. He didn't
even sound angry when he asked me what I thought I was
doing, taking his dog off his property. And he didn't bat
an eyelid when I said I was taking him because he wasn't
any use around the farm. I told him I'd take good care of
the dog, that I'd send him the money for a replacement
just as soon as I'd earned it. I was pleading with him by
then because I could tell what was in his mind. But it
didn't make any difference. He shot the dog, in cold
blood. There was blood in the puddles.'

Jet's long, fined-boned hands came up over her face
and she was trembling uncontrollably as she tried to push
back the memories to the dark silent place inside her
head where she'd locked them away for years.

'The sadistic old bastard!'

Denny's anger touched her as nothing else could have
done at that moment. In some strange way it seemed to
lessen the pain, as if he shared it and in sharing it,
dissipated it until it was at least bearable.

Still shaking, she dropped her hands, meeting his eyes.
She wondered if he knew how the telling of how Prince
died had helped and that he, oddly enough in view of his
loathing for her, was the only person she could possibly
have told.

And then, in the quick flicker of compassion she saw
in his eyes, followed by his low sigh of resignation, she
knew he did understand.

'Some folks certainly know how to hide from trouble!'
Barbie pushed her way through the door, holding the
bucket in one hand and the floor cloth in the other—

cagily hoisted aloft between two fingers. Her eyes swept over the silent couple, not seeing them. She was back on form, pleased with life again, and Jet guessed she and Alan had reached some kind of understanding. Jet envied her. In the end she would probably marry Alan, make him a good wife. The love they would share would be easy and comfortable, it wouldn't make too many demands. It wouldn't be anything like the soaring ecstasy Jet had once known. But there would be no pain . . .

Having disposed of the bucket and cloth, Barbie went to the sink, running the hot tap, vigorously soaping her hands. Jet watched her, not able to dredge up the energy to move, aware of Denny's intent, probing stare.

'Alan and Ben have taken the pup out for a walk, complete with collar and lead. They're trying to train him to walk to heel, or something. They looked so funny—you should have seen them! I told them not to come back until I'd made supper. Gammon and eggs okay? Oh, and I said we'd try to find a roomy cardboard box for Prince to sleep in.' Barbie turned from the sink, her hands dripping, scattering droplets of water over Jet as she reached for the kitchen towel.

Jet rubbed spots of wetness from her face and Barbie stopped in mid-stride, gaping.

'Good grief! You look as if you've been in a road accident! What happened to your clothes?'

Jet looked down at her filthy skirt and blouse then pulled herself stiffly to her feet. She was numb inside, as if her revelations of how the old sheepdog had died, Denny's earlier cruel accusations, his hammering home of the hatred he felt for her, had drained her of the capacity to feel any more.

She wished he would leave, would stop staring at her as if he'd never seen her before and was going to have to

write a detailed descriptive essay on her appearence. She shrugged tiredly.

'Ben fell off the swing on to his nose. It bled a lot and most of it went on me while I was giving him a cuddle to make it better.' Her mouth quirked wryly. 'He's in quite a state himself, or didn't you notice?'

'I noticed!' Barbie opened the fridge door and peered in, moving the milk jug to get at the gammon. 'But it didn't throw me. I'd only start worrying if he came home clean!'

'I'll go and change,' Jet told her, wondering at the oddly reflective look in Denny's eyes. She walked woodenly to the door, but when she heard him say goodbye to Barbie, decline a belatedly offered cup of tea, she increased her pace.

He'd be following her out—he had to, to reach the front door—and the nape of her neck prickled with apprehension because she'd taken as much from him as she could stomach in one day.

'Jet—I have to talk to you.'

His low command halted her as she put one foot on the bottom tread of the staircase. Cursing herself for not having forced her drugged legs to carry her more swiftly up the stairs and out of his reach, before he'd had time to walk through the hall, she squared her shoulders with a visible effort and asked wearily, 'What about?'

They had everything to say to each other, and yet nothing. It would all take too long and she was too tired, and nothing of what she could say to him would make the slightest difference to the way he felt. And that was the saddest thing in the world.

The face she turned to him was grey with defeat, and when she swayed slightly, clutching at the newel post for support, his hand gripped her shoulder, his fingers

biting, a faint frown line appearing between his lowered
dark gold brows.

'We have to talk, Jet,' he told her levelly, the
aggression she had come to see as normal in him in his
dealings with her not in evidence. The warmth of his
fingers on her shoulder reached through the slight
sensation of pain his grip was inflicting. Sickeningly, she
recognised the feelings that licked through her veins and
unfurled in her loins. She craved his nearness, his
touch,—wantonly, mindlessly craved it. Slow, deep
colour flooded her face and she turned her head to hide
the raw need she was sure must show in her eyes.

'I don't think we've anything further to say to each
other,' she muttered thickly. 'You've said it all.'

'We have a great deal to say, Jet.' His hand dropped
back to his side and she instinctively raised her own to
cover the spot where his fingers had been, holding close
the echo of how his touch had felt. 'But not now,
obviously. You look done in.'

His eyes assessed her clinically, as if trying to analyse
her state of defeated wretchedness. Jet could have told
him that the trauma of discovering her heart free of the
imprisoning ice, free at last to admit that she loved him,
had never stopped loving him, had knocked the fight and
determination clean out of her.

She told him no such thing. Whatever happened, he
must not know that her love had never died. She had only
just discovered the truth of her feelings, and the
revelation had shaken her.

'Come down to Tipper's Hollow after you've eaten this
evening. We'll talk then. And don't worry,' he added
gently as her eyes widened with the dismay she felt when
the thought of spending time alone with him made her
wonder just how she would conceal her love from him, 'I
won't attack, verbally or physically, and that's a promise.

I thought I knew you inside out and backwards, but there are a couple of things that don't add up and it's important we talk about it.'

'What things? I don't understand you.' She wanted to creep away, to put distance between them, because every time she looked at him she was remembering the way it felt to be in his arms.

But she was held captive by the magnetic pull of his presence, the indefinable charisma that was part of his attraction. She could no longer trust herself to obey the brain that had for so long overruled her heart, and the knowledge terrified her.

He shrugged, thrusting his hands deep in his side pockets, the action straining the fabric of his trousers tautly across his hard, muscular thighs.

Jet tore her eyes away and he said softly, 'The way your dog died, for one thing. It puts a completely different slant on your uncle's character. And you cared—even now I can see how much you must have cared.' He began to walk away, towards the open front door. 'The way the cold, sophisticated lady messed herself up while cuddling a hurt child, for another. The way that lady gave the child a pet of his own—when I would have staked my life she couldn't stand him near her—for yet another. So, if I've already come across a couple of things that don't add up, there could be a dozen others, for all I know. I'll see you later.'

He had reached the door, his back to her, and he didn't turn when he added softly, meaning every word of it, 'If you don't come under your own steam, Jet, I'll be up here to fetch you.'

# CHAPTER NINE

THE evening was oppressive, the purple air thick and sticky with heat. Even the bats, their tiny shapes reduced to black silhouettes against the ominous sky, seemed sluggish.

Perspiration had gathered wetly on the palms of Jet's hands, and she wiped them irritably on the seat of her trousers, her feet slowing as she left the track and turned to take the short cut to Tipper's Hollow across the bottom of the meadow.

Her taste did not run to the usual uniform of jeans and T-shirt so, when buying casual wear recently, she had chosen a loosely styled scarlet cotton jump-suit, nipped in at the ankles and waist, buttoning up to the collarless neckline. With her silky black hair carefully coiled on the top of her head, she considered she looked sexless, and was confident that her appearance would give Denny no inkling of the way she felt about him. She was totally unaware that her upswept hair drew attention to the appealing length of her fragile neck and left her distinctively beautiful facial bone structure free and uncluttered, her eyes looking enormous, or that the simple garment she wore subtly emphasised the slender female body beneath.

Believing that she had suitably armoured her outer self, she acknowledged she could do little to protect the new vulnerability that was like an aching open wound inside her.

135

Every instinct in her shied away from the coming meeting with Denny. He wanted to talk, but there was nothing to be said. He had made love to her, made promises he had never had any intention of keeping and, six years later, had accused her of killing their child. Three unalterable facts that no words could change. Every meeting between them only increased the pain, gave life to memories better left for dead. And the very worst part of it all was the discovery that her love for him had never died. Despite all that had happened, she loved him still.

She could have refused to go near Tipper's Hollow tonight. It would have been easy enough to drive away, anywhere, stay out of his orbit until he lost interest in hounding her, wounding her, probing her soul with merciless words and even more merciless eyes. She didn't understand his new, softer approach, the dawning gentleness she'd sensed in him when he'd spoken of their need to talk, and she certainly didn't trust it.

But the time for running and hiding was over; what use was evasion when one look from those liquid golden eyes could lay her soul bare? He had sucked her dry of the will to hold herself distant, broken through her defences until she lay open to the insistent pull of his existence. Her feelings for him were a force so powerful that nothing on earth could keep her from him when he called.

She had known that, innocently and instinctively, on that magic-touched night when they had made love. And in all the years, nothing had changed. She had tried, and had believed she had succeeded, to deny him, to block out her feelings for him. But with the melting of her icy defence system she had to admit to the inevitable. In

some strange, frightening way they were still bound together, hating on his part, loving on hers. His will, his sheer masculine magnetism, exerted a pull as timeless and changeless as the moon's dominion over the sea.

Her hand shook as she fumbled with the latch on the wicket gate. The shadowy garden path led to the black bulk of Tipper's Hollow, a medium-sized cottage where muted golden light showed in one open square window.

She took a shuddering breath of the thick night air which was heavy with heat, with the scent of phlox and roses. The atmospheric pressure played on her already heightened senses, a heavy, insistent counterpoint to the nerve-shredding, sharply tugging awareness of Denny's pervasive personality.

She longed, desperately, for the release of the tension, but knew with a sense of fatalistic defeat that there would be no peace for her while she and Denny existed. Even if she put half a world between them he would still be with her, inside her head, filling her heart. She had put him out of her mind once before, but knew she couldn't do it again. She had changed, come back full circle to the girl she had been when she had given her heart, but with an added maturity that denied the use of self-deception.

Jet walked with slow reluctance up the path, her clothes sticking to her in the clammy heat, and quietly, like something in a dream, the door opened, light spilling out along the path, and Denny was there.

Moving towards him like a sleepwalker, she knew she had no power to resist the command that had brought her here, no fight left in her to counter his insults and accusations. They exchanged no greetings; there was no place in their relationship for social trivia.

She followed him through to the sitting-room, her

writer's mind automatically observant. The last time she'd been inside the cottage—climbing in through one of the broken windows—it had been a near ruin. Renovated, it was a snug, compact dwelling, the room they were standing in sparsely furnished, book-lined, essentially masculine. A solitary table lamp shed a pool of amber light, leaving the corners shadowy, and the single window stood open to the night air, the stillness of which did not stir the bitter-brown linen curtains.

The surface of her mind absorbed the information patchily, her inner thoughts revolving in a vortex of blind emotion. He dominated the room, making its contents, its size and shape, insignificant and totally unimportant. She turned to him, the courage that had brought her here to face him hard to hold on to.

The mellow light suited him, softening and melding the fox-shadow hair and deeply tanned skin, turning the yellow of his eyes to glowing gold, giving the illusion of gentleness to a mouth that had become sensually hard over the years. Jet shuddered, suddenly flooded by a sensation of chilliness that came out of nowhere.

He turned wordlessly away, and she heard the clink of glass on glass as she struggled to gain some inner control, to deride the persistent feeling of fate, of destiny. She must not let him see how he affected her. He must never know that the eager, loving innocent of six years ago had finally ousted the cool, hard woman who up until recently had mistakenly believed she had life taped.

Without speaking, his unreadable eyes firmly fixed on her face, he handed her one of the glasses he had carried over. She took it with unsteady fingers, her eyes lifting uneasily from the snugly fitting denims that covered his lean, hard hips to the wide, bony structure of the

shoulders under the black T-shirt he wore. She did not dare meet his eyes: her own would give too much away.

'Sit down, Jet,' he commanded softly, watching the play of emotions on her exquisite, shadowed face, noting her unequal struggle to conceal them.

She moved blindly to a low squashy sofa, sank down on it, then bit into her lower lip, wishing she'd chosen somewhere else, because he joined her, his body heat tangible over the few inches that separated them. Both hands clutched her glass as she shakily raised it to her lips, needing the drink, recognising the brand of the fine old brandy as it slid down, warming the shivery spot deep inside her. She heard his low, husky laugh and looked up to find mocking golden eyes on her, and she blushed furiously as he said, 'I can see you needed that,' feeling gauche and idiotic as he took the empty glass from her, his skin lightly brushing hers, making her shudder as tingling sensation coursed its predictable way through her.

'Relax—I won't bite.'

He rose fluidly, his innate strength and grace moving her unbearably as she watched him refill her glass and place it on a small table within her reach.

The only way to counter her hungry need of him was with simulated anger, and from somewhere she found the strength of mind to toss brittlely, 'Don't tell me your teeth have lost their cutting edge! But if you've forsworn biting, what else do you have in mind?'

'Don't, Jet.' He sat beside her again, leaning back, his eyes holding hers. And if she hadn't known better she would have said there was pain in the sudden darkness that filled them. 'We've fought too often and too furiously. It's high time we both started to think, to talk.'

'Why bother, when you've made it very clear just how much you hate me?' she demanded thickly, the echo of his earlier cruel words flooding her consciousness, blinding her to the quick angry shake of his head, the unsure shrug of hard wide shoulders. 'And, boy, you do hate me, don't you?' she pressed on, needing to fan his anger, to focus on his hatred for her because she was too vulnerable right now to cope with any softening in him.

'I don't know,' he answered surprisingly. He spoke as if he was hurting inside, his eyes closing as if to deny her knowledge of what was going on inside his head. The lines of strain were clearly visible on his hard-boned face as he ground out. 'I don't know, dammit! I've been hating you for so long it's become a habit, feeding on itself, growing fat and ugly. And if I let myself stop hating you, the alternative becomes intolerable!'

'The alternative?' She was visibly trembling, every particle of her being finely tuned to what was going on between them, the interplay of words, the ambiguous shades of meaning—the emotions clear cut, though: hatred, or the long, cold void of nothingness.

'Don't you know?' His question parried hers, his eyes intently held on her shadowed face suddenly dropped to the fine-boned, long-fingered hands that twisted restlessly on her lap, the single smoky stone of the ring she wore catching the light.

'Don't you know, Jet?' he persisted, the words coming harshly, as if demanding her emergence from the brittle shell of her inward thoughts to meet him on the plane he had chosen.

'I only know you give me no peace!' She was unable to hold back the hot words, even though she knew he was drawing her on to some new battleground. Her face felt

tight, the skin dragged back against the bones. 'We once spent twelve hours together, and it's soured up my life ever since.'

The statement was dragged from her, against her will, pulled out by his domination, his need. Her eyes drifted over him, darkening with her sullen acceptance of his power over her, noting how the tightly drawn lines of his face, surprisingly, underlined the pain he was feeling. And again she was tinglingly aware of him, of her own need, her need to give love to this man.

The tension in her prickled to the surface, set her skin crawling, made each small muscle quiver out of control. She drew in a deep breath, twisting her hands together to stop them reaching out for him, only relaxing fractionally when he stood up and moved away with the loose-limbed grace that fascinated her hungry eyes.

Lowering her lids to hide her need, she heard him refill his own glass, then, timeless moments afterwards, he said huskily, 'Tell me why you went away, refused to wait. I want to know everything that's happened to you over the last six years. I have to know.'

'Why?' Pain twisted through her, demanding an outlet. She found it in anger, her cheeks staining a furious red as she bit out, 'You didn't give a damn what happened to me!' She jerked to her feet, unable to sit still. She wanted out. 'What right, what damned right, do you have to demand a post-mortem on my life? You got me pregnant, and six years on you walk back into my life, doing your damnedest to flay me alive! You have no rights, none at all. It's all a game to you, isn't it?' she ground out as he put his body between her and the door she was heading towards, blocking her escape route. 'A sick, evil game!'

Her eyes flashed defiance but her nostrils quivered as she inhaled the heady male scent of him, the faint undertones of the clean lemony aftershave he used. 'You've got a twisted mind, mister, and you turn my stomach!' She was almost crying, her emotions run ragged. 'Six years ago you said we would marry; you never mentioned the little fact that you were engaged to Pamela Trent at the time. And that was the last I saw of you until you came here, throwing every insult in the book, lying about my relationship with Alan, trying to break up my frienship with Barbie! And that gives you rights, does it?'

'Calm down, Jet,' he said quietly. 'God knows, I understand the need to lash out; I've felt it, too. But it won't get us anywhere.'

His expression was unreadable in the shadowy light, but his voice was gentle as he went on patiently, 'As I tried to tell you before, I knew Barbie was getting serious about Alan and I didn't want to see her hurt. I knew you and he had been living at Foundlands, and I couldn't see any man sharing the same roof with you and sleeping in his own bed. And I couldn't see any man, having made love to you, ever being capable of loving another woman.'

Slowly, he placed his hands on her shoulders, his long fingers gentling her. The import of his last words was lost on her as she struggled to fight the weak longing that filled her at his touch; she twisted quickly away, her eyes narrowing to desperate sapphire slits as she spat, 'Don't touch me!'

There was no way she could endure his touch. She wanted it so much and knew nothing could stop the betrayal of her feelings if she allowed the façade of her

anger to break beneath his caressing fingers.

'Very well,' he said calmly. 'I don't want this to degenerate into a slanging match.'

'Why not?' Jet turned sharply on her heel, pacing to the open window. 'It's the only thing you've wanted until now, so why the change of heart? Oh, and if it's of any interest to you, Alan and I have never been lovers. Friends, always. Lovers, never. So you were wrong, weren't you?'

She leaned against the sill, breathing in sticky night air that did nothing to relieve the inner knifing of pain or steady her hammering heartbeats. Thunder rolled in the inky distance and she threw her head back, scenting the air for a hint of the cooling rain that would come with the approaching storm.

His sudden, silent appearance at her side unnerved her, his hand, curving on the soft flesh of her arm, setting her pulses skittering.

'Do storms still terrify you?' His question was softly voiced, carrying an underlying concern, and for a timeless moment their eyes locked and held as shared memories sprang to vivid life—the dusky interior of the shepherd's hut, the fury of the storm that prowled the surrounding hills, the tender, caring man who had gentled the frightened girl. The lovemaking—a wonderful, magical thing that had seemed as natural as breathing, a mating of souls that had demanded the commitment of the ultimate expression of love.

With an effort Jet pulled her eyes away from his as she became aware of the misty softening in them, appalled by the force of the wave of love that engulfed her. He must never know or even guess that the emotion that had been born on the night their child was conceived would

imprison her heart for as long as she lived.

'I grew out of that particular terror,' she muttered edgily, turning to pace restlessly, her arms clasped around her, hugging her body. The tension in her was mounting. If Denny had ever done anything for her it had been to cure her of that pathological fear of thunderstorms, but the cure had been far worse than the disease.

'I want you to tell me one thing, Jet.' His golden eyes were watchful, his deep voice insistent, and she brought her pacings to a slamming halt, her body taut.

'What thing?'

'Why did you say I was engaged to Pamela at the time you and I met?'

He was sitting down now, using a straight-backed chair near the door, his long legs outstretched, his arms hanging loosely at his sides. But beneath the relaxed pose she sensed a tension in him almost as great as her own, and knew that if she tried to go out of that door the tightly leashed energy in him would explode to prevent her doing any such thing.

She resumed her restless pacing across the muted honey-coloured carpet. 'Because the lady in question told me you were,' she bit out at last, the anger and bitterness in her, combined with the dismaying depth of her love for him, producing an explosive amalgam of emotion that demanded release. It came in a flood of words, in an outpouring of things that had never been said, things that could only be said to the man who sat watching, his features impassive, only his glinting golden eyes betraying his intentness. 'I waited for you. I waited for days and I still couldn't make myself believe you'd never come, that you'd taken what you wanted from me and wouldn't

show your face again in a million years!'

Her lips curled in self-derision and she didn't even blink as a vivid flash of lightning flooded the room. Her eyes were blank, back in time, as her feet automatically carried her back and forth across the room.

'So I went to Withington to find you. She told me you were engaged to her. Then I knew you'd never come. I hadn't felt ashamed of what had happened until then.'

Her pacings brought her to the edge of the sofa and she sat down heavily, her eyes inward-looking, remembering how it had felt all those years ago. 'I felt dirty.'

On the periphery of her vision she saw him move, as if he were about to come to her. Dully, through the fog of her own emotions, she saw his features contract in what might have been a spasm of pain, but it was over quickly, his face wiped clean, his voice perfectly relaxed as he said carefully, 'Tell me what happened next. Tell me exactly what happened.'

Jet slammed back to her feet. She wanted to hit him for his clinical impassivity but didn't dare get that close, because if she got close enough to touch him, God only knew what would happen.

She prowled the room restlessly, fingering objects that afterwards, had she been asked, she wouldn't have been able to put a name to.

'What the hell do you think happened?' she snapped, almost at breaking point. 'I broke my heart! I felt like a kid who'd lived her life in a cold dark room, who had briefly seen through an opening door into a world of sunlight and flowers and warmth, only to have the door slammed back in her face and the key turned in the lock and thrown away.' She threw him a hard look, her mouth curling. 'After a while—days, weeks, I don't know—I

began to go around looking for work, for any way I could find of making a living for myself and the dog, away from Micah. But there was nothing.' She rounded on him, bitterness spilling over. 'No one wanted to employ— what was it you called me? "A half-tamed scrubber with hardly a rag to her back"?'

'Jet!' His voice was thick, his eyes darkening with an emotion she couldn't define. He jerked to his feet, his hand staying her. 'Calm down, you're burning yourself out.'

'You're calm enough for the two of us!' She pulled away from him, her face twisted with contempt.

'One of us has to be.' He went to the drinks tray. 'Don't you understand? I have to listen to your side of the story. Then you can hear mine and maybe we'll be able to slot the two sides together and make sense out of it. I'm trying my best to be unemotional about this, and it's not easy, believe me.'

'There's only one side as far as I'm concerned,' Jet dismissed, 'and that's mine. It may sound egocentric of me, but your side could be told in two seconds flat.'

'Just what do you mean?' He had his back to her so she couldn't read his face, but he sounded in control.

Wanting to needle him, to make him show some emotion, even if it was only a tenth of what she was feeling now, she snapped, 'I couldn't be bothered to explain. Your type of man makes me ill!'

Thunder cracked overhead, lightning illuminating the room simultaneously so that she saw him with stark clarity as he turned, and she was seeing again, just for that split second, the man he had been. And to add to that poignant, fleeting impression his voice was warmly caring as he told her, 'Forget what type of man you *think* I

am, Jet. We only need to get at the facts. Sit down, try to relax, and drink this.'

She took the glass of brandy he held out to her, carefully avoiding his fingers, and slumped down on the sofa, stretching her legs out along it so that there'd be no room for him to join her—presuming he wanted to. She knew she had to try to relax, she'd explode if she didn't, and there was no way Denny was going to allow her to leave until he'd found out what he wanted to know.

Outside, the heavens had opened, rain pouring down, hammering on the roof. The curtains at the open window suddenly bellied inwards, bringing an inrush of welcome, cooler air.

Jet sipped her third brandy; she had been too tense to eat the gammon and eggs Barbie had prepared, and the alcohol on an empty stomach was making her feel reckless.

What the hell? Maybe he was right. They had both built pictures in their minds. The one he'd had of her, of a promiscuous tramp living off a string of lovers, bettering her prospects by way of the bedroom, was so off the mark it was laughable!

She closed her eyes, knowing that he was now standing over her, watching her with golden eyes that told her nothing. But it didn't bother her any more. She sipped more brandy, finding the courage to look deliberately for the right words, to strike the right note.

'As I said, I couldn't find work locally and I knew I'd have to try further afield. Then I discovered I was having your child.'

She felt him sit down on the arm of the sofa, near her feet, but she kept her eyes closed. What she had to say concerned him, but she didn't want him to think she was

trying to make him share it. It was too late for sharing now. She had to tell him the facts and get out, carry on with her life, learn to accept the fact of her love for him, live with it instead of hiding it away where it would fester again into the cold hatred that had encased her heart in ice. Taking the brandy in little gulps, as if it were medicine, she elaborated.

'So I stopped looking for work. It was one thing to try to look out for myself and the dog, quite another to care for a child on the little I'd be likely to earn. I knew I'd have to stay with Micah, if only to give the baby a roof over its head. Only Micah didn't see it that way. I told him as soon as I knew myself—I wanted to give him time to get used to the idea before I began to look obviously pregnant.'

'How did he take it?' Denny sounded as if the question came out through gritted teeth and Jet shrugged.

'The way I expected. He called me names, beat me up, and then tried to find out who the father was. I wouldn't tell him, not at first, but I soon picked up the way his mind was working. He wanted to know the father's identity so that he could force a marriage. He went through every name he could think of, starting with Alan, his godson, and ending up with Bill Trotter, the village half-wit. He wouldn't leave it alone. So I told him the truth. I said it was a man I'd met in the hills, someone from London down on holiday. I didn't tell him your name or where you'd been staying. He'd have made trouble for you, and I knew you wouldn't have wanted that,' she finished bitterly, remembering how alone she'd felt, how the old man had gone on and on at her to reveal her lover's name. How, in desperation, she'd said she didn't know, hadn't asked, hadn't seen him before they'd

slept in the hay and wouldn't ever be seeing him again.

Jet drained what was left of the brandy and held the empty glass loosely in her hands, listening to the rain, reliving the awful day when Micah had told her to go, when he'd shot the dog. It had been raining then . . .

'So what happened, Jet?' Denny prompted, his watchful eyes soft with compassion. 'You left, didn't you?'

'Oh yes, I left. He told me to go. His exact words were, "I'm not keeping another man's bastard, so don't think it. Don't come near this place again until you've had it aborted." I hitch-hiked to London. I don't remember much about it; I was too upset about the dog, and worried over how to earn enough to keep myself and the baby——'

'About the abortion, Jet,' Denny interrupted gently, the lines of strain showing clearly on the savagely carved features of his face. 'I can understand now why you felt it was the only way. Micah had thrown you out and you believed I wouldn't come back to you.'

Jet's eyes flew open at his words and she pulled herself upright, the lethargy, the dull emptiness of the last minutes vanished as she grated, 'What abortion? God, what sort of woman do you think I am? No—don't tell me, please don't tell me!'

Her empty glass slid from her fingers, bouncing across the carpet, and Denny, after one long, shocked look, knelt to pick it up, his eyes on a level with hers as he whispered, 'There was no abortion?'

'Of course not!' Sapphire eyes slitted with slightly tipsy scorn. 'I wanted that baby! It was our child. Conceived in love—on my part, anyway.'

She closed her eyes against the sudden hot pricking of

tears, missing the deepening shock that darkened his eyes, pulled the skin taut over his prominent cheekbones.

'Give me some more brandy,' she told him thickly, her throat constricting painfully as she recalled the deep joy she had felt on the day of Tod's birth.

If he disapproved of the way she was knocking his brandy back, he didn't show it, and she was grateful for that. The rest of the story had to be told, and she had gone too far to hold anything back. OK, so he hadn't cared what had become of her, hadn't given her a second thought until somehow, somewhere, he'd learned how Tod had died. But Tod had been his son, so he had the right to know.

She had faced a lot in her life and if, in the end, he still accused her of killing their child, she would face that too. Though why he should ask if she'd had an abortion when he knew she hadn't, she couldn't imagine. She wrinkled her brow in an effort to concentrate, but her mind was clouded with brandy fumes and she gave up the attempt because what she was going to have to tell him next was filling her mind so that nothing else could get a look-in.

His fingers were shaking slightly as he gave her the brandy she'd asked for, and she noticed the dark stain of sweat on the front of his sleeveless vest. The air had cooled considerably since the storm had broken, so it couldn't be the heat that was making him sweat. Moisture glistened on the golden skin covering his lean, muscular shoulders and on the tawny hair on his strong male arms and she wanted those arms holding her, keeping her safe on her journey through the dark land of memory.

She shuddered, wishing she hadn't touched the alcohol; it was making her muddled, increasing her

vulnerability where he was concerned. She had to remember how much he hated her, impress that unalterable fact firmly on her mind, because if she forgot it for an instant she would be crawling into his arms, begging for his love.

'How did you make out? Where did you live?' Denny's voice cut through her hazy thoughts, his presence a powerful force, and she knew, tiredly, that she had to get the words out, satisfy his probing curiousity, before he would give her the peace she needed to get her world on an even keel again.

'I eventually found myself in a back-street café somewhere in Islington,' she told him listlessly. 'I sat there for ages, wondering what to do. It was dark—late— they were closing, they said. Then one of the waitresses started talking to me, and she got the sorry story out of me—I was broke, homeless and pregnant.'

She heard his harsh intake of breath and her eyes followed him as he walked over to the open window, his shoulders hunched as he stared out into the night. It was easier to talk when he wasn't watching her, and she went on, the words almost falling over each other in her need to get them out before he turned back to her, began watching her again.

'The girl, Denise, told me they were short of a waitress for the evening shift. She usually did days, she said, and she'd try to fix me up with the job so she could get back to her normal routine. She was kind—rough and ready, but kind. And I got the job and I moved in with her. She had a place nearby, a couple of rooms and the use of a kitchen. After the baby was born I took a job at a local pub because the pay was that little bit better. I still worked evenings so that I could be at home in the

daytime, and Denise looked after him while I was working. If she went out I paid the old lady who lived on the floor below us to come in. Anyway, I started writing short stories, and they sold. I liked doing it and the extra money helped buy things—a full-sized cot, baby clothes—you know.' She shivered, clamping her lips together. He didn't know. He couldn't know how hard it had been, or how worthwhile, or how much joy she'd found in her love for Tod.

'Where is our son now?' His words, carried to her on the damp, scented night air rocked her mind. How could he be so cruel? He knew Tod was dead! He knew! He'd accused her of killing him, so he had to know!

'Where do you think?' She was gasping for breath, her speech ragged, the pressure inside her head intolerable. She wished she didn't love him, wished she still believed she hated him, because it was easier, so much easier!

'Tell me.'

She shot a hard look at his rigid back, the broad shoulders held high, and she whipped herself to anger because it was the easiest thing to do and she could cope with that.

'I'm doing my best to tell you! And when I've told you, I'm going, and I'm never setting eyes on you again because you're driving me out of my mind!'

'Then tell me.'

He might have been talking to a stranger; there was nothing in his voice but a flat emptiness, and Jet curled her hands into fists and ground out slowly, 'When he was eighteen months old I had a letter from the fiction editor of the magazine which published my short stories. He wanted to discuss the possibility of my writing a serial. I was over the moon; I really felt I was getting somewhere.

Really proud of myself.' Her voice grew progressively flatter. 'He asked me to go and see him on the Monday afternoon. I didn't want to take the baby; he'd had a cold and the weather was bitter. Denise said she'd take a day off work, look after him for me, have a few friends in to keep her company. So I went.'

Suddenly her voice rose, and the shaking harshness of it had Denny slewing round, his eyes narrowing as she covered her face with her hands, screaming at him, 'So you were right, I was responsible! I should have taken him with me. If he'd been with me he wouldn't have died in the fire!'

'What fire? For God's sake, Jet, what fire?'

She hadn't heard him come to her, but she felt his hands tearing hers away from her face, and her wild eyes fastened on his deeply shocked gaze, her mouth working uncontrollably as she gasped, 'When I came back our room had been gutted by fire and my baby was dead. She'd thrown a party, asked all her out-of-work friends in. They'd lit an old paraffin stove because the place was cold. Someone had knocked it over, and if I hadn't left him, or if I'd taken him with me, or if I'd hurried back sooner instead of trying to sell myself and my silly romantic story ideas to that editor, our son would be alive today. So yes, you were right. I killed him; it was all my fault!'

She was shouting hysterically, out of control, and Denny, his face ashen, slapped her once, producing a stillness that kept her upright and rigid and silent for a second or two until he pulled her, sobbing and weak, into the protective circle of his arms.

Jet cried as she had never cried before. She hadn't shed a tear when she'd been told that Tod had been dead

before the fire crew had managed to bring him out of the room. She had been turned to stone, and stones don't cry.

Taking her grief for her baby, her guilt and horror over the way he had died, the love for Denny she still clung on to—romantically and foolishly—she had parcelled them up and locked them out of her life, because if she hadn't done that she would have gone insane.

In the years since her baby's death she hadn't spoken of these things or allowed herself to think of them, and now, because of meeting Denny again, everything had been dragged out, and she'd been forced to face them, and nothing would ever be the same again.

# CHAPTER TEN

'WHAT was his name?'

She was cried out now, and she had no idea how long he had held her as she'd shed the tears that should have fallen in the days and weeks following Tod's death, weeks when she had existed in a black limbo of emptiness, her shock too deep to admit the healing quality of tears.

Jet lifted her head from where it rested against his chest, the feel of his warmth lingering on her cheek as, trembling slightly, she met his eyes. They were wet with tears, too, and the sight of them hurt her unbearably. She wanted to take his grief away. She had never felt closer to him than at this moment.

Later he might restate his earlier accusations, let his hatred of her show again, but for now she could only try to give him ease in the way that his gentleness, while she had sobbed in his arms for all they had had and all they had lost, had eased her.

'His name was Tod Luellyn,' she whispered unsteadily, aching inside for love of the tawny-haired, mature-eyed man who held her so tenderly. 'He took my surname, of course, and I called him Tod because it was the nearest I could get to yours. "Tod" is an old Scottish name for fox, you see.'

Her words trembled away to nothing as she saw the raw emotion in his eyes. And when he bowed his bright head, laying his forehead on her shoulder, she felt the hot

wetness of his tears against the cool skin of her neck and her arms tightened around him.

She needed to offer him comfort—the deep love she bore him demanded that. But she would never get through to him on that plane. Her irresponsible behaviour in leaving Tod with Denise when she'd known the girl was planning a party of sorts had lost him the son he had never known. She stood not only accused by him but by the guilt that had festered inside her for so long, so how could she possibly give comfort?

'He had your eyes,' she told him softly, offering what little she could. 'And my hair. He was a beautiful boy,' she added brokenly, feeling the convulsive shudder that racked his body, hearing the effort he made for control as he told her,

'I want to know everything there is to know about my son. Tell me, Jet. I have to feel I know him.'

He talked as if Tod were still alive, she thought raggedly. She remembered once reading, somewhere, that no one died as long as they still lived in another person's thoughts. She would make Tod live in Denny's mind as surely as he now lived in her memory. It was the only thing she could do for him.

Very gently, he led her to the sofa, cradling her in his arms. And curled against him, his nearness melting her, the closeness they were sharing softening away the last crumbling vestiges of the icy wall she had erected around her heart, the wall she had believed to be impenetrable, she told him all she could, every tiny detail, reliving their child's brief span of life.

Jet knew this was a moment out of time. Sooner or later he would be back to hating her again. But she would be able to handle it. It would no longer produce the edgy,

uncomprehending fear she had lived with since he'd come back into her life, because now she understood it.

He must have read an account of the fire that had killed Tod; the more sensational newspapers had had a field day, placing great emphasis on the crazy party, the fact that the dead child's mother had been out at the time, making her sound giddy, or worse.

His hatred must have started at that moment and she hadn't told him a thing to lessen it, but for the moment there was a truce, a quietness that healed them both.

Giving an account of the last six years of her life had been far from easy, but his indomitable will had dragged the words from her, and she knew she had been able to tell him nothing to lessen the resentment he still must feel. So when his husky voice told her, 'You have nothing in the world to feel guilty about, Jet,' she stiffened in disbelief.

Then, slowly, she twisted into a kneeling position on the sofa at his side, brushing the tangle of loosened hair back from her face, watching him with wary, questioning eyes.

He looked tired, lines of strain etched deeply around his eyes, but his mouth was softly moulded with a gentleness that pulled her apart with longing. And sadness. She knew the softening in him had everything to do with what she had told him about Tod and nothing whatever to do with his feelings for her. Despite his amazing statement that she had no need to feel guilty, she knew he could have heard nothing to make him change his original opinion.

'You were doing what you thought best for Tod,' he said in response to the perplexity in her eyes. 'You were trying to bring in a better income. And you left him at

home, with someone you knew to look after him, which was the best any mother could do in the circumstances.'

He reached for her hands, his fingers twining with hers, and his eyes were drenched with an emotion she didn't understand as he said thickly, 'If we're going to allocate blame—and I know in my heart we can't—then it's more mine than yours.'

'Yours?' His hands were gripping hers so tightly she had to bite her lips to stop herself from crying out with the pain he was unknowingly inflicting. There was something here she didn't understand, and she knew it was important. 'Yours?' she prompted urgently.

'If I'd found you sooner, if I hadn't put the wrong construction on what that girl said, if I'd waited instead of blasting off, building up hatred brick by damned brick, then I could have saved my son where those drunks at the party couldn't.'

He sounded as if he were in torment, and Jet whispered, 'Denny, please tell me what you're talking about. What girl? What did she tell you?'

'I went to the place where you lived,' replied Denny slowly. 'And from what you've told me, it must have been the day of the fire. It had taken me that long to track you down.' He shook his head, his eyes heavy with regret. 'I can remember the squalid flight of stairs to the flat I'd been told you were sharing as well as if I'd walked up them yesterday. A big, tarty-looking blond girl opened the door.'

'Denise.' Jet's heart hammered, beating against her rib cage. He had come looking for her on the one day she was out. Frustration coiled inside her, tightening impossibly as Denny nodded, his lips pulled back against his teeth.

'Must have been. It was about four in the afternoon

and there was already one hell of a party going on. I could hear music, laughter, voices—all loud. I asked to see you and she told me you were out with a chap.'

'The magazine editor,' injected Jet, feeling drained.

'Obviously. Though I didn't know that at the time. I knew nothing except that it all tied up with what your uncle had told me. It all added up—the squalid place you were living in, the sleazy flat-mate, the drunken party, you being "out with a chap". No, Jet,' he released her hands suddenly, sagging back against the sofa, his eyes closed, 'if I'd gone in and waited—she did ask me if I wanted to—instead of putting the wrong interpretation on everything, Tod could be alive. You weren't to blame.'

He looked flaked out. Jet longed to take that beloved face between her hands and kiss away the ageing lines of self-recrimination. But it would be the last thing he needed from her, and so she reminded him cautiously, 'You told me I was. To blame, I mean.'

'And I could sentence myself to a lingering death for saying that!' he ground out desperately, the hands that had been lying loosely at his sides clenching to fists, the knuckles showing white beneath the tanned skin. 'I wanted to punish you, and go on punishing you, God help me! I believed what Micah had told me, that you'd had our child aborted. God—when I think of what I've put you through! I swear I'll never take anything on face value again, Jet, I swear it!'

He turned bleak eyes to her, and she knew that the hating had stopped, that the man who had haunted her, slaying her with his bitter words, had gone.

It was too late now, of course, she accepted that. Six years was a long time, and if he'd cared for her once it was over now. That she still loved him, with an intensity

she scarcely dared think about, was something she'd have to come to terms with. But he had cared, a little, because although he hadn't come for her when he'd promised he would, he'd obviously sought her out later, and having heard from Micah that she was pregnant, had taken the trouble to track her down.

'What exactly did Micah tell you?' she asked quietly, holding his eyes, wondering at the savage flicker that turned them to molten gold before dying, leaving them bleakly cold as he stated,

'I went to Foundlands as soon as I could after getting back to England. You obviously know nothing about the letter I asked Mrs Briggs to deliver to you personally.'

Jet shook her head, completely bewildered, and Denny took a deep breath.

'No, I guessed as much from what you've told me. You see, when I arrived back at Withington Manor that day, Pam told me my paper had been trying to reach me. I rang through and was told I was booked out on a flight late that afternoon—some trouble spot in East Africa—and I was to cover the story, stay with it until recalled. There wasn't time to get to you, so I wrote a letter, explaining, promising to get to you as soon as I could. I gave it to Mrs Briggs and asked her to walk over with it that afternoon. Your uncle, apparently, wasn't on the phone, and I had to get a message to you somehow.'

'Alan said he only had the phone put in about a year before he died,' Jet murmured, 'and I didn't get any letter.'

'I know that now. But when I went for you, I couldn't understand why you hadn't waited. I was desperate to see you again. I was worried in case you'd had second thoughts, worried in case you'd feel as I was beginning to

feel, that our meeting and loving was unreal, dreamlike. It was only when Micah told me you'd gone and wouldn't be back, that I knew it hadn't been a dream—it hurt too damn much for that.

'You weren't there, Jet, and Micah wasn't saying where you could be found. He refused to tell me anything at all until I loosened his tongue with a couple of tenners. Then he told me you'd gone away to have an abortion. The father had been some man you'd met in the hills— you'd always been a "dirty stop-out". And in his opinion, you'd turn pro; you'd been staying out at nights for long enough, getting up to the lord only knew what with the local lads——'

'It wasn't like that,' Jet interrupted dully, unable to rake up any fury against the hateful old man who had been her unwilling, uncaring guardian.

'I know.' He leaned forward, his arms lying along the length of his thighs, his hands dangling. He gave her a long sideways look, his mouth bitter. 'I didn't want to believe that of you. But I had to believe what he told me about your condition, and a lot of women regard abortion as commonplace these days. I can't describe the way I felt when I thought about you getting rid of our child, not even waiting until I got back. I asked discreet questions in the village but the feedback I got bore out what Micah had said. Young Jet Luellyn was half wild . . . spent most of her time, when she wasn't working, up in the hills . . . stopping out for days at a stretch when she got the chance . . . Goodness only knew what would become of her . . . And so on, and so on. So I spent the next five or six years hating you, vowing that one day I'd find you and make you pay for what you'd put me through. It was the abortion-that-never-was that I was referring to when I

said you'd killed our child.' He drew in a harsh, shuddering breath. 'Can you ever forgive me for the abuse I've handed out?'

He sounded tired, as if there was nothing left in him but a hopeless weariness, a defeat of the spirit that took him away from her more surely than his bitter recriminations had ever done. She nodded, unable to speak, and the impression of emptiness was endorsed when he got slowly to his feet, looking down at her with unreadable eyes.

'There's no point in going over dead ground, is there? It's all over. Come, Jet.' He held out a hand, his eyes softening. 'You're out on your feet. Time you were tucked up in bed.'

He took her hand, pulling her to her feet. Her legs felt unsteady and she wanted to cry because he'd never said a truer word when he'd told her it was all over. It was, for him. No loving, no hating. Nothing. And now he was asking her, kindly, to leave. He would need tonight, or what was left of it, to come to terms with what he'd learned, and then he'd be able to go on from there because he was strong and single minded. But where to? To Pamela Trent? Very probably. Or someone like her. There would be room in his heart now for other things. Hating her, as he had done, must have taken all the space there was.

'You haven't taken in a word I've been saying, have you, Jet?'

She looked up, her dazed eyes meeting his, finding concerned compassion. She shook her head. She hadn't been hearing him. She wanted to tell him not to worry about her, she'd be fine, just fine, but he was telling her again, 'You can stay here. There's no point in going back

to Foundlands. I'll phone through and tell Barbie not to expect you. You can have my bed; I'll kip down in the spare room.'

She could hardly raise the energy to nod her agreement, and certainly couldn't dredge up enough to argue about it. What did it matter where she slept? She sighed, the effort of doing even that suddenly almost too much for her.

His former weariness seemed to have disappeared and he was showing the caring, supportive side of his character that she would have given anything to experience during those long, worrying months before Tod's birth.

He half carried her up the narrow stairs, suiting his pace to her faltering steps, his arm tightly held around her waist. Weakly, she wanted nothing more than to lean against him, craving the love he no longer had to give.

His bedroom was square, and the double bed took up most of the floor space. He eased her down on to the edge of the duvet-covered mattress, his hands a gentle pressure on her shoulders as he advised, 'Get some sleep. We'll talk some more in the morning.' Leaving her, he pulled fresh pyjamas out of a chest of drawers and put them into her still, heavy-feeling hands. 'Use these. I'll bring you some hot milk.'

When he had gone she stared at the closed door for a long time before she realised she was crying. Swift, hot tears she couldn't stop coursed down her cheeks. He had forced his way back into her mind and heart, hacking away the ice that had kept her safe. And he would never leave her now because wherever he was she would still be loving him. There was no retreat to the cold, distant place she had inhabited since the fire that had taken her son.

The door was opened carefully and the sight of Denny, balancing a beaker of hot milk and a plate of neatly cut sandwiches on a tray—complete with an embroidered cloth—threw her utterly.

She couldn't take this evidence of the gentler, caring side of him; his hatred had been almost easier to bear because then she'd had her own to combat it; now all she had left was a love that was tearing her apart, piece by piece.

'Jet... Oh, Jet, my sweet!' The carefully prepared tray was unceremoniously dumped on the floor as his raking glance took in the signs of her distress, and he was on the bed beside her, holding her, his fingers splayed in the midnight darkness of her hair as he pulled her head against his shoulder. 'Don't cry, baby, don't. I can't take it!'

The very real note of anguish in his voice helped her to get back some control. She hated herself for being so weak, for inflicting her weakness on him. The last thing she wanted was his pity or that he should feel in any way responsible for the wretched tears she kept flooding him with.

'Sorry.' She knuckled her eyes, as if trying to push the tears back where they belonged, out of sight. 'I'm fine now, truly. It's all been a bit—a bit traumatic,' she told him shakily.

'Sure it has.' Two strong hands curved gently round her face, amber eyes searching, the lines of anxiety easing away as she gave him a wobbly smile.

'That's my girl!' His own eyes crinkled at the corners, the tiny indentations gradually smoothing out as his gaze dropped lingeringly over her face and rested on her lips.

She knew he was going to kiss her, and her bones

melted with the longing only he could invoke. Without thought, her lips parted, trembling slightly, as his mouth dropped to take hers, offering him the sweet moistness within willingly. He could take as little or as much as he needed because everything she had was his. She loved him with every last vestige of the deep passion she had denied for so long, and this was all she would ever have of him.

Gradually he deepened the kiss, and fire flooded her veins as she savoured the pleasure his mouth was giving. Her hands went up to seek the crisp hair at the nape of his neck, her fingers finding the hard bone beneath the rich pelt of hair.

Moaning her need, she pushed closer to him, her breasts hard and full against his steely male body. Questing, wandering hands found the warmth of the smooth skin of his back beneath the vest, and she felt a convulsive shudder ripple through him, and then he was pulling her down with him until they lay side by side on the bed.

'Denny . . .' She whispered his name like a prayer, her lips moving slowly and sensually beneath his, and he softly took his mouth from hers, watching her intently from eyes of burning gold as his fingers began working on the buttons of her jumpsuit.

'Denny . . . Yes. Please, yes!' She answered his unspoken question, all her love, her need, showing in the intense brilliance of deep sapphire eyes. The desire she felt for him had been smothered for too long; there was no way she could deny him now. No way she would want to. This act of lovemaking would become a memory of him she would treasure and hold through the empty years of her future. It needed no other justification than that.

He was shaking now with the force of his wanting, the tremors setting tiny ripples running over his bronzed skin like the path of a small breeze over placid waters. A soft smile curved her lips to tender perfection as she helped him with the buttons, a tenderness for him that held her own desire momentarily in check, a need to give that transcended all else.

And then she was lying naked, relaxed on his bed, the dark mass of her hair spread out against the soft pillows, offering herself to him. She heard him groan and she put her hands on his chest, feeling the dampness of his skin beneath her palms. Then he was kissing her, tasting every inch of her satin-smooth body until the need he invoked was too great to be borne.

'Love me, Denny,' she pleaded breathlessly, the pleasure he was giving her with his lips and hands making her want to cry out with the sheer beauty of it.

'You know I will.' His voice was throaty, his movements rapid as he shrugged out of his clothing, removing the last barrier between them. She had time to drink in the virile masculinity of his hard male body before he moved over her, staring deeply into her eyes as he held his body in check above her thighs.

'I've waited for this moment for so long, Jet,' he muttered thickly. 'So very long, my sweet.'

Convulsively, she reached up to him and he slipped slowly and deliberately between her legs, his eyes rimmed with fire, commanding hers.

'Look at me, Jet. Tell me you've ached for me as I've ached for you. Look at me. Tell me!'

She told him, her voice lost in the thunder of her own heartbeats, her senses focused on the soaring love she gave him as she matched, stroke for stroke, the slow,

lingering, tasting thrusts of his body.

'We've both wanted this . . . and this . . . for so long . . . so many years.' His voice was husky, his eyes holding hers as if he could reach inside her soul as surely as he reached inside her body until his hunger could be contained no longer and Jet knew, as his control slipped, that this night's lovemaking transcended anything she had ever dreamed possible.

She had loved him at eighteen, wildly and devotedly, but it was a woman's love she gave him now and it was stronger, purer, for the fire it had had to pass through before meeting this moment of truth.

She woke early; the small clock on the bedside table read five past six. Easing herself out of bed, taking care not to wake Denny, she stood looking at him for several long minutes, her eyes drenched with love.

Their lovemaking had been perfect. Time and again he had taken her, as if he couldn't have enough of her, and she had responded to his gentle, erotically teasing arousal of her body with a passion that had left them both shaken.

He was sprawled out now, deeply asleep, and her heart constricted painfully because she knew the magic was over. Last night had been a fantasy, a dream-like conclusion to the trauma of what had gone before, an outlet for emotions that had become heightened through grief and regret to something that demanded an overpowering release.

A necessary fantasy for him but total reality for her, the only reality there would be in the years to come. Sunlight from the open window caressed his close-cropped hair, turning it a rich liquid gold, touched his

perfect body, relaxed and fluid in sleep. The lines of strain had been washed from his strongly beautiful features and his smile was peaceful.

It took all her willpower to prevent herself from climbing back on that bed, twining her arms around his naked body and pulling his beloved head to the softness of her breasts.

Steeling herself against the temptation that was tugging her towards him, she dressed quickly, buttoning herself into her crumpled jumpsuit, pushing her feet into her sneakers. She would have a shower and change her clothes when she got back to Foundlands; no one would be up and about at this time in the morning. She needed to be on her own for a while, so she would leave a note for Barbie and take herself off into the hills. She had to look the rest of her life straight in the eye, plan what to do.

She didn't look at Denny again; she couldn't trust herself not to linger, not to resort to feeble tears again if she did. Saying goodbye would be painful, and she'd said her silent farewells to him after he'd fallen asleep, holding her, just before dawn.

Her hand was already grasping the front door latch when she changed her mind about leaving without any kind of word for him. There had been no disguising his anguish last night when he'd realised just how badly he'd misjudged her. She didn't want him to worry about her.

Almost reluctantly, she pattered back to the sitting-room and began to search for paper and something to write with. She just needed to leave a few words, something casual and friendly: 'See you some time, Denny. I'm glad everthing finally got sorted out and don't give me another thought, I'm fine.' Something like that should do, should be enough to stop him worrying

about her, feeling responsible for her because of what
had happened over the past six years.

'Hi—early bird.'

His lazy, yawning words held her rigid, her back to the
door where he had entered too quietly to have given her
any warning.

To meet him face to face was the last thing she wanted
right now. Their loving had been so perfect. She didn't
want his apologies or his goodbyes, his concern, to stand
in her memory between last night and their separate
futures. But she had to act as if everything was fine and
dandy.

She turned, the shock of his nearness filling her. He
was naked except for a towel he'd hitched precariously
around his waist, leaning against the doorframe, half
asleep still.

'I reached out for you and you weren't there.' He
rasped a hand along the side of his lean cheek, fingering
the stubble almost absent-mindedly, his golden eyes full
of tenderness, his mouth a soft, sleepy curve. 'Come back
to bed, sweetheart.'

'Sorry!' Her heart slammed violently but she didn't let
it show; she even achieved a cheerful ring to her voice.
She turned her head, making a pretence of securing the
window he hadn't properly fastened last night, so that he
shouldn't see the pain in her eyes. 'I've got a busy day
ahead of me, a thousand and one things to do.'

'Oh.' He sounded flat for just a moment, but there was
a smile in his voice as he added, 'Pity. I was looking
forward to a nice long lie-in! Still,' he came further into
the room, smiling widely, waking up, 'it's probably for
the best. If we went back to bed now we wouldn't surface
again for days, and I've got a planning conference to get

to—you'd be amazed at the work I've let slide these last weeks!'

'Right.' She flashed him a big bright smile, wondering how she could do it when her heart was breaking up with love for him. 'Then you'd better get a move on. Me, too.'

'You've got time to make coffee.' It was a statement, not a question, and she knew the old Denny was back—in command, but gently this time. He would always be gentle in his dealings with her now, she knew that, and it only made her love him more.

She was about to refuse, to laugh and tell him to make his own—she was a working woman with a living to make. But she hesitated too long and he was telling her, 'You'll find the coffee and the filter jug in the kitchen. Eggs, too, if you're hungry. I'll have mine scrambled,' he grinned, tossing over a broad tanned shoulder, 'if you've decided we've both got to work today I'll get dressed and shaved. Because,' his eyes darkened to topaz, 'because if I stay here any longer I'll sure as hell override your decision!'

She watched him go, knowing just how he felt because it wouldn't take much persuasion on his part to get her back in his bed. He would only need to touch her, to say he wanted her . . .

Last night had been a time out of this world, a time when sensible decisions had had no part, like the need to separate and forget the past, the sane reasoning that told her he had to be given the freedom to go his own way, get on with a life that had no real place in it for her and hadn't done for the last six years.

But last night could not be repeated. There was only so much she could take without breaking down and confessing her love for him. If he knew she had always

loved him and always would, he would feel trapped by the past, by his sense of responsibility. She would not subject him to that; she loved him too much.

The coffee had brewed, the almond-green cups and matching plates were on the plain pine table under the window, and Jet was just piling fluffy eggs on to buttered toast when Denny walked in.

He had shaved and showered and looked alert and fresh, carrying an aura of power as easily as he wore his superbly cut dark grey business suit and crisp white shirt with a deep olive green silk tie.

Jet's heart did a double flip, assaulted by the overwhelming masculinity that was not one iota lessened by the formal elegance of his attire.

He smiled with his eyes, his mouth still softened by the aftermath of their tempestuous lovemaking, and Jet sat down quickly, before she fell, and said in a voice she tried to make cheerfully crisp but which came out sharply acid, 'Eat, before it gets cold.'

Her hands were shaking as she poured coffee for them both, and she picked up her own cup quickly, gulping at the hot reviving brew, enduring the way it scalded its way down her throat because it did a little to help block out her awareness of him.

'You're not eating?' He was standing over her, making no attempt to have his meal, and she shook her head swiftly, her tumbled hair hiding her face. 'You should. Don't make me worry about you more than I already do, Jet.'

The deep concern in his voice was like a slowly turning knife, and she struggled hard to find the composure to make some flip, throwaway remark, but wasn't given the

time because he bent over her, pushing the hair back from her face.

Gently he put a hand on either side of her head, lifting it, his eyes searching hers with a tenderness that had her own sparkling with the brilliance of unshed tears.

The balls of his thumbs moved softly against her prominently defined cheekbones as he lowered his head to tease her lips apart with his, his tongue erotically tasting the honeyed sweetness of her inner lips.

Desire stirred fiercely inside her and the whimper in her throat turned to a sob as he raised his mouth, whispering, every soft word searing her mind, 'I shall have to stay away for two or three days, sweetheart, but I'll be back with a special licence in my pocket. We'll be married, Jet. Six years too late, I'm afraid. But I'll make it all up to you somehow, that I promise.'

# CHAPTER ELEVEN

SHE hadn't been prepared for that. For his concern, yes, for a watching friendship that would drive her crazy because she wanted far more than that, yes again. But a proposal of marriage—never!

'Have you nothing to say?' He lifted her chin, forcing her to look at him, and the smile, the warmth in his eyes, had her trembling, on the brink of thoughtless capitulation. But she must not capitulate, ever; she could not allow him to honour a promise made six years ago simply because he pitied her. 'We could have a quiet ceremony in the village church. Will you contact the vicar, or would you prefer me to do it?'

What on earth could she say! Had he loved her she would have hurled herself into his arms, delirious with happiness. But to accept him, knowing that he didn't love her, that the bond that would tie him to her would be nothing more than pity and a misplaced sense of responsibility, would be sentencing them both to a lifetime of regret. She couldn't do it to him, or to herself, and she could hardly come right out with it and tell him he didn't *have* to marry her. It would be throwing his compassion, his good intentions, back in his face.

The new maturity she'd bought, at such cost, over the last weeks, the change in her that had enabled her to at last face up to her memories and emotions, helped her now.

'Six years is a long time, Denny,' she told him levelly.

'We're both different people.'

'We're older and wiser,' he agreed, matching her tone, the mood she'd set. He pulled out a chair and faced her across the table, the breakfast she'd made for him ignored. 'But surely, that's no bad thing? We've both been through hell, in our different ways, and we've earned our slice of heaven, especially you.'

And that was it in a nutshell. He was offering to make it up to her, to care for her as no one else had ever done since the death of her parents. And it wasn't enough, could never be enough, for either of them.

Jet closed her eyes briefly, hiding the stress his quiet words produced. And when she lifted her long, sweeping lashes and forced herself to meet his warm, watching eyes she knew how to play it.

'I'd have married you six years ago like a shot,' she said lightly. 'I was very young, incredibly innocent, and I couldn't remember what it felt like to be loved. But I've grown up since then, made my own life.' She shrugged slightly, trying to smile. 'I've found out what I like doing—writing—and I've been fortunate enough to make a great deal of money from it. I'm free and independent and that's the way I like it.'

She struggled to find the right words to convince him that he need not feel he owed her anything, and thought she'd found them when she said lightly, 'I don't want to tie myself down or make any long-term commitments to anyone.'

But he argued, a frown cutting a deep line between his eyes, 'I can understand that, Jet. The people you've relied on in the past have let you down in their different ways: your parents—though it was hardly their fault—that brutal, sadistic uncle, Denise with her irresponsibility

and myself—though letting you down was the last thing I meant to do. So I can understand why you don't want to put your happiness in anyone's hands. But I'd make you happy, Jet. I would never let you down.'

'It isn't that,' she said gruffly, wishing he'd leave it alone, take her refusal and be thankful! 'I've told you—I've grown up. I'll never again expect or want my future security or happiness to be the result of anyone's actions but my own. Please try to understand, Denny. I can't marry you.'

She looked at him with empty eyes and caught the angry, puzzled light in his.

'Is it because you don't trust me? Because you've seen me with Pam?' He leaned forward, his hands reaching for hers across the table, his eyes more serious than she'd ever seen them as he stated, 'I was never, at any time, remotely interested in Pam Trent—much less engaged to her. I know she was—shall we say—infatuated with me at one time, but I did nothing to encourage her. She's simply the daughter of very dear friends. And I'll make her retract that lie she told, if it'll clear your mind. And I'll find out why the letter I gave Mrs Briggs to deliver to you never arrived. You do believe I wrote it, don't you?'

She returned the pressure of his hands briefly before pulling her own away, puzzled by the pleading intensity of his eyes. Surely she had told him enough to allow him to believe she didn't need the selfless act of reparation his offer of marriage entailed?

'And last night, Jet,' he continued remorselessly, his voice deepening to a husky intimacy that melted her bones. 'You can't tell me it didn't mean anything to you, that you'd make love with any passably presentable man.'

Jet scrambled to her feet, setting the table rocking. She couldn't talk about last night; it had meant all the world to her, but he musn't know that. But her self-respect wouldn't let her lie; what had happened between them was too precious for her to sully with lies that could lead him to believe she was the promiscuous tramp he'd thought her to be only a few short hours ago. She wouldn't defile her love for him in that way.

'Last night meant a great deal to me, you know that,' she told him shakily. 'You are the only man who has ever made love to me, got near me in any way. But it isn't enough. Being good in bed together is not enough to base a marriage on. There has to be love.'

As she turned blindly for the door she heard him groan, the sound wrenched from deep inside him.

'Is there someone else? Tell me, Jet!'

She turned reluctantly, not seeing the tightly leashed emotion in him, seeing only the questioning, slightly puzzled surface expression as he put his hands round his cooling cup of coffee.

'No, there's no one else.' She looked at him with sad quiet eyes. 'There's no one I want to marry, now or ever.'

The house seemed very quiet, unnaturally so. Barbie and Ben had gone to stay with Alan for the weekend, taking Prince because Ben refused to be parted from the pup any more than he had to be. Leaving him behind when he went to school was bad enough.

Autumn colours were already turning the trees to gold, and the air had a discernible chill to it that made Jet think about log fires, warm sweaters and long dark nights when she would sit alone and make a start on a new novel.

The last Roger Blye book had been finished, not without difficulty, and there wouldn't be another. The content of the books held no appeal for her now. The brilliant hardness of the mind that had produced them had softened, making the conception of further hard-bitten crime novels impossible.

When she wrote again it would be something softer, gentler. Jet knew she would probably suffer financially; the demise of Roger Blye would make a hole in her income that Jet Luellyn, aspiring romantic novelist, probably wouldn't be able to fill. But she had the courage to face up to that possibility, just as she had found the courage to face a life alone, without Denny, but loving him still.

She hadn't seen him since the day she had refused to marry him. Tipper's Hollow was deserted, rank weeds growing among the flower plantings, the once neatly trimmed lawn looking like an overgrown meadow.

There was no reason for him to return; their drama had been played out. He had his career, based in London, a circle of friends of whom she knew nothing, a life of his own to live. He was free to do that now, free of the hating resentment that had brought him here, time after time, knowing she would return one day. Free of the feeling of responsibility that had come when he'd learned the truth. She had let him know that he had no need to feel in any way responsible for her, and he was sensible enough to leave it at that. If he came back at all it would be to collect his belongings from the cottage, although, for all she knew, he might have already done that. Every day she expected to hear there was a For Sale board near the wicket outside Tipper's Hollow.

Jet sighed, giving herself a mental shake. It was no use

brooding. Picking up a hairbrush, she began to stroke it through her recently washed hair. Barbie and Alan were planning to marry at Christmas and then she would be completely alone, except for her memories. She wondered, idly, if she would start keeping cats—dozens of them—and wearing strange hats and talking to herself!

A giggle bubbled to the surface at the absurdity of the picture her mind was conjuring up, and she tossed the brush on to the dressing table and stood up, hitching the belt of her bathrobe more tightly around her waist, shivering a little. It was growing dark outside and there was definitely a nip in the air.

She padded quickly to the window and leant out to grab the clasp, intending to close it, shocked to stillness as she heard him call her name.

Held rigid, wondering if she was hearing things, already beginning to go mad, she searched the gathering twilight with wide eyes, her long hair falling forwards, brushing the sill.

'You look like Rapunzel.'

She saw him standing at the corner of the house, staring up at her, his face a pale, unreadable blur in the dark amethyst air. Unconsciously, a wide smile lit her face as he moved forwards, his hands outstretched in what would have seemed, if she hadn't known better, to be entreaty as he asked gruffly, 'Aren't you going to come down and let me in?'

'Of course!' It was a job to get the words out, her heart was beating so thickly, but she ran from the room and down the stairs as if she had wings on her feet. She tried to remind herself that he had probably only called by to tell her that he was putting his cottage up for sale, had come to collect his things and say goodbye. But her heart

was beating its own ungovernable tattoo, and no amount of reasoning could diminish her joy at seeing him again— even though she knew that seeing him could only bring more pain.

A swift look in the mirror above the hall table told her the worst. She looked like a woman who was going to her lover! Huge eyes sparkled above flushed cheeks, her lips were soft, parted on a half smile that wouldn't go away no matter how hard she tried to straighten it out, and her hair was a softly dark wild mass that seemed, of its own accord, to be inviting a lover's tender fingers.

It simply wouldn't do! No matter how happy she felt at the prospect of seeing him, talking to him, even if only for a little while, she must not let him see it.

So she settled what she hoped was a polite but friendly mask on her face, took a deep breath to steady the trembling that shuddered through her, and opened the door.

He was leaning against the frame, totally relaxed, his features blank. He was wearing a light, roll-necked cashmere sweater in a colour that matched his tawny eyes and charcoal-grey cord jeans that fitted his lean hips and long legs to snug perfection.

Jet's heart turned over with an electrifying flip and she held the door open, stepping backwards, babbling, 'Do come in. Are you down for the weekend? You only just caught me—I was going to make an early night of it.'

She led the way through to the sitting-room, knowing she sounded like a fool—or the eccentric spinster she had so recently conjured to mind, thrown into confusion by a male caller! But there was nothing she could do about it, because her tongue seemed to have a life of its own, and as she flicked on lights, marching full tilt into the centre

of the room, she heard herself twittering, 'Barbie's over at Alan's place—with Ben, of course. They'll be getting married at Christmas, did you know? Oh, sorry, can I get you a drink? Coffee, or something stronger?'

She reached into the drinks cupboard and pulled out the first bottle her fingers made contact with, twisting round but not looking at him as she gabbled, 'Did you have a good journey down? The roads can be hell on a Friday evening——'

'Shut up, Jet.'

His words were quiet but effective, and the edgy excitement that had produced the inane babbling drained out of her and she fell silent, meeting his eyes for the first time, finding them unreadable.

He took the bottle from her fingers and placed it on a low table. It was red wine, and he said, 'Maybe we'll open it later. We'll see how it goes.'

What that was supposed to mean she didn't know, but she did what he suggested with a flick of his hand, and sat down.

Without saying anything he went to lean against the window-sill, half sitting, his arms crossed over his chest. She had never seen him look quite so bland and businesslike; emotion, in one form or another, had always been beween them previously.

'I have something to say to you, Jet, and I want you to hear me out,' he began soberly. 'To begin with, just to set the record straight, I want you to know that Pam told you that she and I were engaged because she was jealous. I'd told her and her parents—who not unnaturally wanted to know where I'd been the previous night—that you and I had met, fallen in love, and were to be married. Apparently, when she found Mrs Briggs with the letter

I'd given her, Pam said she'd take it because she knew all about it and wanted to have a word with you in any case about "hanging around me" and "making a nuisance of yourself".

'I'm telling you this because I don't want you to believe that I didn't do everything I could to let you know what was going on when I was sent out to East Africa. Do you believe me, or do you want me to take you over to see Pam now so that you can hear it from the horse's mouth? It wasn't pleasant, getting the truth out of her, but for your sake I'll make her spell it out again.'

Jet shook her head wordlessly, regretting his need to rake over the past. It made everything so much worse when she thought how the jealous, spiteful actions of one woman had led to so much misery.

'Right. And for my part I know that you kept faith, that far from being the little tramp your uncle led me to believe you were—only too eager to have an unwanted pregnancy ended—you made as good a life as you could for our child against soul-destroying odds.'

His voice sounded clipped, as if he were addressing a board meeting, and Jet shivered, making a movement towards the bottle of wine, needing something to sustain her through this new ordeal he was putting her through.

'Later.' The shake of his head, the brusqueness of his command, had her slumping back in her seat.

Speaking around the lump in her throat, she asked, 'What *is* this all about? We both know, now, what really happened—why go over it again?'

'Because it's important. It leads up to what I'm about to say. Knowing that neither of us was to blame for what happened means that there's no cause for resentment, on either side. Agreed?' He didn't wait for any reply she

might have made, but clipped on, 'Neither of us has formed a lasting attachment for anyone else during the years we've been apart, and while I can accept that you aren't still in love with me—you said you couldn't marry without love, as I recall—I do believe we could build a very satisfactory relationship. The physical attraction's there, neither of us can deny that, and because of what happened six years ago, the child who came out of our loving, there's a deep bond between us.'

'Are you suggesting, again, that we marry?' whispered Jet, appalled by the singularly cold-blooded way he was going about it. At least the last time he had asked her it had been done with the warmth of his concern for her wellbeing!

'I am.' He was not at all put out by the way she shot to her feet, frowning at him, scrabbling in the drinks cupboard. She found a corkscrew and held it and the bottle of wine out to him, muttering tersely,

'Open it, for medicinal reasons if nothing else—I think I need it!'

She reached for glasses, not knowing whether she wanted to laugh or cry. And while she held the glasses as he filled them with the dark, rich wine she told him levelly, 'We've talked round this before and my answer's still the same. Heavens above, Denny, why are you so keen to tie us together in a loveless marriage? You must have masochistic leanings I haven't noticed before!'

'I am trying to make a rational proposition,' he snapped, turning back to the window, staring out into the darkness, his powerful shoulder muscles bunched up beneath the thin covering of cashmere. 'But I'm finding it remarkably difficult, faced by your flippancy!'

So she was being flippant now, was she? Jet slumped

back in the armchair and sipped wine moodily. How was she supposed to behave? Faint? Throw a fit? Crawl on her knees in gratitude for what he was offering? Because what he was offering, if only he offered his love to go with it, was enough to make her want to do all three!

'Why does the idea of marriage frighten you?' he asked at last, turning, walking closer. 'Don't answer—I'll tell you. Because, as you pointed out, you have a successful career.' He came closer still, his golden eyes intent on her troubled sapphire gaze. 'You have your own home, a lifestyle that's tailor-made, and your independence.'

He stood over her, close enough for Jet to see the golden tips on his dark lashes, the pulse that throbbed uncertainly at the base of his throat, betraying the fact that he was not quite as controlled as he would like her to believe he was.

'Fine,' he said heavily. 'I appreciate all that. And what I have in mind wouldn't make much difference to any of it. Marry me, and we'll both have companionship, a belonging together. I won't infringe on your career and I won't expect you to take any interest in mine. During the week I'll be in London, working, living at my apartment. You will live here, get on with your work in peace. I'll join you at weekends. I won't make any demands you're not prepared to meet. Will you think about it?'

'No!'

The answer came immediately. It was as much as she could do not to hurl the contents of her glass in his face. It was the best recipe for marital disaster she'd heard of yet! Total non-involvement in the important day-to-day career areas of each partner's life, the two of them only coming together at weekends for some vaguely defined companionship—and bed!

It might work between partners who entered, clear-headedly, into a loveless marriage, and the trouble was, she reflected miserably, that was precisely the sort of marriage he had in mind. Though why, she was unable to fathom. He was attractive, far beyond the norm, intelligent, warm—he could have his pick of women only too willing to be his wife, the pick of women to fall in love with.

'I hope that's not your final word on the subject.'

She sensed the tension in him as he stood over her and she was about to tell him it was, and would he please change the subject; when he said stiffly, 'I'm asking you to think about it, Jet, very carefully. I'll go now.'

He didn't look at her as he walked to the door and when he reached it he stood facing it, his back firmly turned on her as he said, 'I'll come back next weekend, after you've had time to re-consider. I'm not going to beg ...' His voice was suddenly lost on a long, indrawn breath and the raw anguish in his voice stunned her as he slammed round, his face drawn. 'But I am begging, Jet! For the first time in my life I'm begging for something I can't live without—can't find!'

'Denny!' He was hurting and she couldn't calmly sit and watch. Here was a man who was deeply troubled, torn apart—for all the pains he had taken to hide it from her. His clipped, detached manner had only been a front to hide his pain from her. She should heve seen through it sooner—she loved him, didn't she!

She ran to him then and held him in her arms, comforting him with the warmth of her love. He laid his head against hers, whispering brokenly, 'I love you so much, Jet. I'm begging you to give me part of yourself. I want all of you, God knows I do,' he groaned thickly, 'but

I'll settle for as much as you want to give—even if it's only the right to call you my wife, share your bed and board at weekends. Maybe I don't rate much with you, not after the way I treated you, but I know you care a little. That night we spent together told me that, and it was something I'll never forget as long as I live. We seemed like two parts of a whole, and without you I'm going to be less than half a man—less than half alive!'

'You love me? You *are* sure about that?'

Incredulity, joy, lifted her voice to something that approached a cry of pain and he drew away from her, holding her gently by her shoulders, the eyes probing hers darkly intent as he said quickly, 'I've never been so sure of anything! I've always loved you. For me, it didn't die. I tried to tell myself I hated you, but deep in my heart I knew it wasn't true. The feeling I had for you had to be translated into something less killing than the pain of loving you, losing you.'

He pulled her close, his hands softly caressing her back, the warm vibrancy of his touch penetrating the thin silk of her robe.

'Why do you think I haunted this place, even to the extent of buying the cottage and spending all my spare time there? I even wanted to buy Foundlands because once you had lived here!' he murmured huskily, his lips brushing her cheeks, and she knew that, physically, he was holding himself in check, her closeness affecting him as his was affecting her. 'Why do you think I reacted so violently when I saw you again? I was insane with a jealousy I didn't know how to cope with because I thought Alan was your lover. And it drove me on to lash out at you, again and again, hurting you in every way I knew how.'

She couldn't speak; there was a lump in her throat that threatened to choke her and she could feel her heart drumming against his as, gently, he cupped her face with hands that were shaking a little, looking deep into her eyes.

'Don't tell me there's nothing left for you at all,' he pleaded. 'Tell me I have a chance.'

'I can't take it in!' The smile she tried out was wavery, spiced with the tears that deepened the brilliance of her eyes. 'You blast your way back into my life, vowing eternal hatred. Then you offer to marry me, out of pity——'

'Never pity, Jet.' He wiped away a solitary falling tear with the ball of his thumb. 'And never hatred—for all the hot words. It was an act of self-defence because when I finally found you again my emotions blew up. There you were, temporarily living here with Alan—or so I thought. Cool, utterly beautiful, completely in control of yourself. The frightened, loving girl-child of the hills had grown up with a vengeance—grown up and away from me. You left me in no doubt that you wouldn't give me the time of day and I knew I'd lost you then. Then, much later, I realised that you weren't as hard as you tried to appear. You could still feel hurt over the death of a dog and you weren't above getting yourself all messed up while cuddling a hurt child. I knew I still loved you then, had never stopped loving you, and I made up my mind that I'd get the truth out of you, and even if it turned out that you'd aborted our child, had had dozens of lovers, I'd ask you to marry me and try to make you fall in love with me again.'

Jet buried her head in his chest, too choked up inside to do more than murmur his name, and he held her,

tenderness in his voice as he entreated again, 'Can't we try, Jet? These last weeks have been hell. I tried to accept your refusal, God knows I did, but everywhere I looked I saw your face and I knew I had to have one more try.'

'Tell me again that you love me,' she whispered hesitantly, scarcely able to take the truth in, even now.

'Always. I'll always love you, Jet. Even if you send me away.'

His arms tightened possessively, crushing her body against his, and she lifted her face to him trustingly, her joy showing clearly in the look of love she gave him as she murmured softly, 'I'll never send you away again. I love you. It didn't die for me, either. I felt like I'd been through an earthquake when the truth of it hit me, and I've been shaking ever since. Hold me,' she pleaded huskily as she heard his sudden intake of breath, felt the tremor of happiness surge through him.

His lips found hers, gently parting them. She had been about to tell him she would marry him tomorrow, but she surrendered herself to the magic of his embrace as their kiss deepened mutually, deliciously ... She would tell him in the morning ...

# Take 4 best-selling love stories FREE
## Plus get a FREE surprise gift!

# ATTRACTIVE, SPACE SAVING BOOK RACK

Display your most prized novels on this handsome and sturdy book rack. The hand-rubbed walnut finish will blend into your library decor with quiet elegance, providing a practical organizer for your favorite hard-or soft-covered books.

**Only $9.95**

*Approximately 16" x 8" when assembled*

*Assembles in seconds!*

---

To order, rush your name, address and zip code, along with a check or money order for $10.70* ($9.95 plus 75¢ postage and handling) payable to *Harlequin Reader Service*:

Harlequin Reader Service
Book Rack Offer
901 Fuhrmann Blvd.
P.O. Box 1325
Buffalo, NY 14269-1325

*Offer not available in Canada.*

*New York residents add appropriate sales tax.

BKR-1R